Meltin

Cyborg Seduction - Book Three

By Laurann Dohner

Melting Iron

by Laurann Dohner

Being a female mechanic on a space station for eight years has taught Dawn a lot of tough life lessons that have hardened her heart. She's got a temper and a mouth to match her red hair and has never backed away from a challenge. Then she's kidnapped and blackmailed into agreeing to be a cyborg's personal sex slave.

Iron is one big bastard with long, fiery red hair, intense, dark blue eyes and a stubborn streak as thick as his dense muscles. If Iron thinks he can tame her, he's about to learn that "meek" is not in Dawn's vocabulary. But with that handsome face, a body to die for, a wickedly talented tongue and those magical hands, the guy just doesn't fight fair.

Dawn is intent on melting Iron's icy resolve to never fall in love with a human. He's winning her heart and she's determined to win his right back. These two redheads have just met their matches. Let the battle for love begin.

Cyborg Seduction Series

Melting Iron

Copyright © August 2016

Editor: Kelli Collins

Cover Art: Dar Albert

eBook ISBN: 978-1-944526-70-2

Dedication

To Mr. Laurann — the man who won my heart and keeps me happy.

Chapter One

Not knowing what would happen to her was the worst. Dawn swallowed the water from the bottle she held in her hand, studying Cathy. They were the last two women left in the cage. Five women had been shoved into the large cell but in the past few days, three of them had been taken away one at a time.

"It's going to be fine," Dawn lied. "They are ransoming us. That's why they come and take us one at a time."

Cathy was young, just twenty, new to outer space, the harshness of it, and terrified. "You really think so? Earth will pay theses pirates for us, right?"

Dawn hated lying, but she wanted to comfort the younger woman, so she just nodded. She couldn't say that big of a lie aloud knowing that Earth Government wouldn't pay money for lowly, off-world workers. The men who had boarded their shuttle to take them weren't pirates. Dawn was certain of what they really were. She'd heard the stories, had talked to witnesses firsthand, and their metallic-colored skin was a dead giveaway.

"Okay," Cathy sniffed. "Thanks, Dawn. I'm really afraid. I thought those men took our co-workers away to kill them."

Terror ate at her. She couldn't glance at Cathy again without revealing it. Dawn looked away to stare through the bars at the small cargo area where the cage had been placed. It was a ten-by-ten-foot cage with solid bars. Sleeping bags had been tossed in, along with some food and water. The only other addition was a portable toilet in the corner. There was another smaller cage in the room, an empty one that had housed an injured woman not from their shuttle but kidnapped from somewhere else. They'd taken her away too.

The men who'd boarded the shuttle were all over six-feet tall, had varying shades of metallic-gray skin, but looked human. Some pirates were radiation-mutated humans who refused to live on Earth or the other governed colonies. Living in space on old ships was dangerous long term, and radiation leaks on them were common under those conditions, poisoning and mutating all life aboard. They weren't really sane, for the most part, and in a civilized setting they would have been imprisoned for their unstable behavior. Space pirates were usually considered the worst of humanity.

But the large gray men were something far worse.

Dawn had worked at the Vonder Station for eight years. It was a deep space station that orbited Arian Nine, a carbon-based planet that was nearing humanoid life standards, thanks to a lot of hard work. Arian Nine had low oxygen content so for those years Dawn had overseen the maintenance of the machines that produced mass vegetation plantation on the surface. The oxygen levels had slowly increased and were now just a year away from being stable for colonization. In all that time Dawn had traveled back and forth between Earth and the Vonder and had heard the stories passed around by the crews of the many space vessels. And she knew a little of the history of their creation on her home planet. Those big gray men were cyborgs.

Dawn almost whimpered as she studied the cargo area again. The ship she was on was the *Rally*. Once, two years ago, she'd been on this very jumper shuttle, doing the welding. She stared up at the blast doors, knowing it was her work.

The *Rally* had sent a distress signal to Vonder Station, saying they'd been attacked by cyborgs. For the three days they'd been aboard the station, the survivors had told horror stories they'd heard during their travels. It was rumored that the gray-skinned monsters were body-parts stealers who kidnapped humans to harvest them for spare parts. They had been lucky to escape with their lives.

The *Rally* had been crippled still when it had left Vonder Station but it had been patched up enough to make it back to Earth. Unfortunately, it had disappeared in space. Now Dawn knew what had happened to it.

Hot tears filled her eyes but she blinked them back. She'd welded that very wall where it had been damaged, to seal the rupture and make the cargo area sound. The cyborgs had obviously waited for the *Rally* to leave Vonder Station to attack it again. She could guess the fate of the shuttle's crew since the cyborgs had captured the *Rally*. Her fate would be the same as those men. She was destined to be killed for spare parts.

"Do you think we'll be ransomed soon?" Cathy sounded less frightened.

Dawn forced a smile while she turned toward the younger, clueless woman. "I'm sure it's all going to be over very soon. Just think happy thoughts, kiddo."

"I'm going to get some shuteye. I'm wiped out."

Dawn watched her settle down but then her attention returned to the weld scar of her repair. It was ironic that she'd patched the same shuttle that now held her prisoner.

* * * * *

The doors opened to the main area of the shuttle. Dawn tensed, her gaze automatically going to Cathy, who still slept. Dawn stood to glare at the tall, black-haired cyborg who walked in. He met her anger-filled gaze before his focus fixed on Cathy as he reached for the keys on his belt.

Dawn moved between him and the other girl. "Take me instead."

The cyborg frowned and opened the door as their gazes met. The cyborg was a light-skinned male with hair chopped short to his head and dark brown eyes. He was at least six-foot-one, wide shouldered, and muscular. All of the cyborgs she'd seen so far wore black leather uniforms with heavy-duty black boots.

"No. I want her. Move aside. If you try to escape, you won't get far."

Dawn tensed in anger. At thirty-six she was in good shape. She'd had to be to do her job for eight years. Her work was very physically demanding. She pulled twelve- to fourteen-hour shifts to keep the equipment going, spending months at a time on Vonder Station. Sometimes, if she'd needed the money bad enough, she'd spent six-month stretches working, then a few weeks on Earth for a break before she returned to her shifts again.

"I said, take me. This is her first time in space and she's innocent. She doesn't know what you are and she has no idea what's in store for her. Please." Dawn took a step toward him. "Take me instead."

10

The man ran his gaze up and down her body. "You're too small for what I am looking for. Besides, one has already claimed you. He will come for you later when Doc has time to do the procedure. Move aside."

A shiver of horror slid down Dawn's spine. She could imagine what kind of procedure some doctor was going to do to her, literally portioning out her ass. She wondered how many pieces of her would be divided up between cyborgs in need of fresh organs, tissue, and whatever else they used.

She was going to die anyway and Cathy was too. Dawn had wanted to buy the girl a few more hours of peace before reality became a nightmare but that time was now up. The man wanted Cathy but Dawn wasn't about to let him take the girl while she was still alive. Cathy was her new assistant and Dawn was responsible for her. She'd even promised the girl's father over the vid screen that she'd watch out for her as if Cathy were her own. Dawn tensed her body, preparing herself for the worst. She'd keep her word to the end.

"Move aside," the cyborg ordered.

Dawn nodded and turned, pretending to comply. She kicked out suddenly, bending at the waist to throw her foot back and nailed the unsuspecting cyborg dead in the crotch. She was grateful that they hadn't taken her footwear when they'd captured her. She had metal in the soles and toes of her boots because some parts of the station had unstable gravity so they'd magnetized the hulls. She heard the man gasp. Dawn spun and kicked out again. Her boot made contact with his face as he doubled over and the blow sent him flying backward, out of the cage.

11

Dawn moved fast as he hit the floor hard, not wanting to give him time to recover. She left the cage and used her boot to kick the man again in the head. He rolled from the force of the blow and grunted. He was facedown, unmoving, out cold, as she stood over him panting. At five-foot-four, no one ever saw her as a threat. As a supervisor, she'd had to learn to fight. Women could be as mean as men, and far out in space, sometimes the only way to handle insubordination was a good ass kicking. She bent over to grab the keys from his hand.

Dawn glanced at Cathy and confirmed the girl still slept. Exhaustion, terror, and buckets of tears had made her sleep as if she were dead. Dawn closed her eyes and mentally pictured the inside of the *Rally*. Two years ago was a long time but she remembered that the large shuttle hadn't had an escape pod. Most jumper shuttles carried one but the *Rally* hadn't because they'd lost theirs in the first attack from the cyborgs before they'd made it to the station. It would be in this cargo area if they had replaced it.

There was no escape. She'd counted five cyborgs on board but the shuttle could hold twenty. It would be tight living quarters but it was possible. She opened her eyes to study the blast doors. Beyond them were the docking port doors. One wall on the other side of the docking port was all that kept the shuttle from being exposed to space. She walked to the blast doors and prayed that no one had changed the access imprints she'd been granted when she'd done the patch work. Relief was instant as the thick doors slid open when her hand touched the pad.

She stepped into the smaller room that contained the docking doors that led to outer space. She couldn't take out the entire shuttle but she could end one cyborg's life and she could save Cathy from being tortured

12

while they cut her apart. It was a kinder way to die to have oxygen sucked out while the girl slept. A queasy feeling made bile rise in Dawn's throat but she swallowed it down. She wasn't a killer but she was about to end three lives. It was horrifying but the alternative was worse—to be cut up for spare parts.

Making her decision, Dawn stepped into the room and turned to study the emergency cutting equipment stored on the wall. She gripped the handle of the crowbar and tore it down to wedge the blast doors open so they wouldn't shut after she removed the cutting torch. She grabbed the torch and pushed the igniter button. A hot flame shot from the tip of the tool.

She heard a door open in the cargo area and turned, recognizing the redheaded cyborg as one of the men who had kidnapped her and taken away the injured woman from the other cage. He was a big bastard, at least six-feet-three with fiery red hair in a tight braid that reached his ass. His hair was starkly evident against his burnished metallic-colored skin and black clothes. He walked forward then froze as he frowned at the downed cyborg on the floor. The big man stared in shock at him then his gaze flew to the open cage door. He quickly scanned the area and she saw his blue eyes widen when they locked on her.

She smiled at him. "I'll see you in hell." She lifted the torch.

"Don't," he roared.

She smelled the metal burning as she held the hot flame to the outer door. In seconds the specialized torch would burn through the thick steel and all hell would break loose when the hull breached.

13

The man started to move, but instead of turning to escape the cargo area, the crazy son of a bitch rushed at her. Alarms screamed as the sensors picked up the danger while the metal heated. The blast doors tried to shut from the docking port but instead they hit the metal bar that wedged them open.

She feared the torch wouldn't cut all the way through before the big cyborg reached her. She knew she had breached the hull when the sound of a blaring alarm pierced the room.

The big cyborg literally dove through the opening of the door to hit her body. Her thumb jerked off the igniter button as it flew out of her hand and she slammed hard into the wall when he tackled her. Pain exploded through her body and something heavy crushed her when she landed on the floor.

The heavy weight on top of her moved as the man roared out a curse over the alarm. Something gripped her wrist, the only warning she had before suddenly being out from under the crushing weight. She screamed as pain tore through her shoulder and arm. Her body was lifted and thrown. She was weightless for a second before she slammed hard into the solid, unforgiving floor of the cargo area.

She hit the deck with a grunt and rolled. Her eyes opened to see the big redheaded cyborg jerk on the crowbar that kept the blast door open. The bar broke loose, the blast doors slammed shut and the alarms went quiet. The sudden silence was eerie.

Terror hit Dawn. The man had gotten them both out of the docking area and had closed off the cargo area in seconds. There was no way those doors would open now since the hull had been breached on the other side, even with access. It was a safety feature that couldn't be overridden. The large cyborg turned to face her, rage in his eyes as he threw the bar away. It bounced off something metal, clanked as it landed and then his mouth opened.

"What the hell is wrong with you? You could have killed us all!" His voice was harsh and deep.

She blinked at him but said nothing as she evaluated her injures. Her shoulder hurt, her hip throbbed, her arm hurt from where the cyborg had gripped it to throw her out of the way and her body ached from the hard landing. She struggled to sit up, to give him the dirtiest look she could manage while in pain.

"That was the plan."

He actually growled. Anger turned the metallic-gray tone of his skin darker around his cheeks. His full lips slammed together when his furious gaze went to the downed cyborg while he moved toward the man. The cyborg's large boots boomed as he stomped across the deck to kneel and feel for a pulse. His head jerked up and his dark blue eyes glared into Dawn's.

"If you'd killed him, they would demand your death on Garden. Don't ever take a risk like that again. You belong to me." He straightened, his fists balled at his sides. "Do you understand me? You are mine and you will obey me."

She stared at him in shock. "What?"

"You heard me."

A sob broke the silence as Dawn stared at the enraged male glaring at her. Dawn turned her head to stare at Cathy. The woman was huddled in the corner, staring back at her, making her want to flinch at Cathy's terrified and horrified expression, both emotions directed at Dawn.

"Why?" Cathy's voice broke. "Why did you try to kill us?"

Regret twisted Dawn's gut as she studied the naïve girl. "They aren't pirates. They are cyborgs. I didn't want you to suffer. Please don't look at me like I'm a monster. I was only trying to do the humanitarian thing for us both."

"I don't understand. You said they were going to ransom us. You're insane." Cathy's tear-filled gaze flew to the cyborg. "Please put me in the other cage away from her. She's lost her mind."

The downed cyborg groaned and lifted his chin, reaching for the side of his skull while rubbing the back of it. He shook his head and then tensed. For a big man he could move fast. He was on his feet in a heartbeat. He glared at Dawn and then his gaze took in the scene in the cargo area. He turned toward the redheaded cyborg.

"Iron, she attacked me. What happened after I was out?"

"She opened the blasting doors, used the crowbar to jam them and then used the cutting torch to breach the outer hull in the docking port." The redhead glared at the other man. "She damn near killed us all. How did she get the drop on you? She's tiny."

"She can fight." The man glared at Dawn. "Attack me now, human. I am prepared so you won't fool me twice with your small body and weak appearance."

"Shut up, Vollus," Iron snapped. "She got the drop on you. The hull ruptured so the docking doors are useless until we repair them." His focus landed on Dawn. "What I want to know is how you got those doors open in the first place. You aren't big enough to drag his body to the scanner and you don't have access to open the doors."

Dawn crossed her arms over her chest and pressed her lips tightly together. She wasn't going to tell him anything. He could just—

Cathy sniffed. "She repairs everything on Vonder Station and fixes the planting equipment that is sent down to the planet. She's the mechanic. She is also good with electronics. She can get any door open."

"Shut up, Cathy." Dawn got to her feet, shrugging off her injures, sure they were just a few bruises. "They don't care about that. They just care about how healthy we are. They are cyborgs."

"I don't understand," Cathy whispered.

Dawn turned to glare at the redheaded cyborg named Iron. "How about we make a deal? You make deals, don't you?"

The man cocked his head as his eyes narrowed. "You want to make a deal?"

She nodded. "If you let her go safely and alive, untouched and totally as is, I'll repair anything wrong on the *Rally*. I'll work for you if you swear you won't harm her. I'm really skilled." She paused. "I can patch the hole I just created."

He frowned. "We do our own repairs. We don't need a mechanic."

Dawn wanted to curse. "All right. How about this? You and I will fight. If I win, you let her go."

The big redheaded cyborg blinked. His mouth opened and a deep chuckle escaped his lips. "Is that a joke?"

Dawn shook her head. "No joke. If I win the fight, you let her go unharmed."

"We have no intention of—"

Iron cut the other cyborg off. "Shut up, Vollus." He grinned, shaking his head. "I have no interest in beating up a fragile human in an unfair fight. One hit and you'd be in a med bed."

Frustration welled in Dawn. "Name what you want for her life."

"They are going to ransom us," Cathy said. "You told me that."

Dawn turned her head to eye Cathy. "I lied. I didn't want you to know what they were really going to do to you. They are cyborgs. They..." She sighed. "It won't be good, okay? I tried to prevent it but that plan didn't work out." She turned her head to glare at Iron. "Name what you want for her life. Is there any humanity left in you? Look at her, she's a good kid. She doesn't deserve to die out here like this."

Iron wasn't amused anymore. He arched an eyebrow. "And you do deserve to die out in space?"

Dawn hesitated. "I've learned all the risks out here and I stayed knowing what I was facing. She's clueless and innocent. Name what you want if you don't need me to do repairs."

Iron tilted his head, watching her closely. "I swear she won't be killed or harmed if you become my personal slave."

Surprise tore through Dawn. She hadn't expected that. "Your slave?"

The big man nodded. "My slave. You follow my orders and do everything I tell you to do." He moved closer, looking down at her. "Everything I want."

"You'll let her go free the first chance you come across another ship heading to a safe port, or Earth, if I agree?"

"No." He shook his head. "But she won't be harmed and she'll live."

Dawn shook her head. "No. That's not good enough."

Iron frowned at her. "That's the deal. She'll be alive and..." His blue eyes glittered with amusement. "She'll stay whole. That's what you're afraid of, correct? That we are going to use your bodies for spare parts? Gut you while you're alive and screaming to take what we want?"

Cathy gasped. Dawn flinched, swallowing hard. She glared at the cyborg, knowing her bargaining power was almost zilch.

"What will happen to her exactly if I agree to this? I want to know what she'll be in for."

Iron turned his head toward the other cyborg. "You're sexually attracted to the other one, correct?"

Vollus glanced at Cathy. He nodded and looked back at Iron. "Yes."

Iron looked at Dawn. "I'll give her to him. She'll live with him and provide sex but he won't harm her."

Shock tore through Dawn. She stared at the large men. They were big, thickly muscled, and from what she understood, cyborgs were mechanically enhanced. They were basically super humans. They had sex? That was a frightening thought. It put a whole new spin on why Iron wanted her for a slave. She shivered. Did that mean he'd want to have sex with her?

19

The other cyborg nodded. "I won't harm her."

Dawn looked over the man she'd attacked. He was big, but not as big as the redhead. "Just you? You won't let the other cyborgs at her?"

He shook his head. "Just myself. I will treat her well and I will not injure her in any way."

Cathy sobbed, the sound making Dawn inwardly cringe. It was a better fate than death. The man wasn't going to whore Cathy out, if he could be believed, and he was saying he wouldn't abuse her. Her attention went back to Iron. She found herself nodding. She'd do whatever it took to save Cathy from being cut up.

"Deal."

Chapter Two

Iron had brought her to a small room in the crew quarters. He'd let her use the toilet and then he'd tied her down on the bed, leaving her alone for hours to worry about her fate. When the doors opened, filled with dread, she watched the big cyborg walk in.

"We are moving to my quarters on the *Star*." He had a really deep voice.

"What's that?"

"A class-A cruiser."

Shock rolled through her. "Earth designed?"

He untied her and gripped her arm so she couldn't get away. "Yes. They were able to dock with us and repair the damage you did." He sounded pissed off. "You won't be given another opportunity to cause trouble. I will punish you if you pull another stunt. You are my slave. I still control the other human so she will pay as well if you misbehave or embarrass me in any way."

Anger surged as she glared up at him. "You're an asshole."

His eyes narrowed. He gripped her arm and pulled her along to the cargo area. The docking door had been welded to seal the damage she'd done. The docking sleeve was extended, allowing them to walk onto the other ship. She was led through a huge cargo hold. From the size of it, she knew the cyborg hadn't lied about the classification of the *Star*. He took her to a lift and they shot up nine floors, letting her know for sure it a big ship.

He then led her down a corridor. She saw that all the doors were spaced close together, cluing her in that they were on a deck of crew quarters.

His room was decent sized, beating the closet she had on the Vonder. This one had a bed, a cleansing room with a top-of-the-line foam cleansing unit and there was even some spare floor space to walk around the room. Not a lot, but enough. On the Vonder, she had a shelf in the wall that had a slide-down door for privacy. The cleansing room was shared by thirty other sleeping compartments and they used rubbing gel to get clean. When the door closed behind them, the large cyborg glared down at her.

"Remove your clothing."

She took a deep breath. "Just like that, huh? No getting to know each other first? No dinner and a vid?" She paused, knowing she was totally being a smartass. "Don't I at least get replicated flowers?"

He blinked at her, a frown curving his lips downward. "I want you naked on my bed."

Her gaze went to his bed as she swallowed the lump that formed in her throat. Her heart pounded almost painfully. She'd made a deal with the big cyborg to be his slave. He obviously wanted to fuck her. Her attention shifted back to him, taking him in from head to foot. He had to weigh at least two fifty, maybe more, with that massive frame. His arms were solid muscle. She nodded while inching away from him to put a little more space between them.

Her hands shook as she removed her jumpsuit. As much as she hated the brightly colored one-piece outfit, this was the first time she dreaded taking it off. She unzipped it slowly while her gaze roamed the room, looking for a weapon. She might not have dated or had sex with a man in a few years but this wasn't her idea of a way to finally break her dry spell. Cyborgs had never factored into her sexual fantasies.

She stripped down to her undergarments and then turned fully to face the large man. He was standing in the exact position, hadn't moved an inch from when she'd turned away from him. Their gazes locked.

"I said remove all of your clothing. I want you naked and stretched out on my bed on your back for me."

Frowning, she glared at him as she jerkily removed her undergarments, shivering from the chilly ship air that the cyborg didn't seem to notice. Maybe the cold didn't bother him since he hadn't adjusted his living quarter's controls. The room had to be in the high sixties, not really freezing but definitely chillier than Dawn liked. Her nipples tightened as goose bumps rose on her skin. She lifted her chin while she kept her fists to her sides. She fought the urge to cover her bared breasts even as his dark blue gaze lowered from her face to her chest.

His mouth tensed and she saw his Adam's apple move as he swallowed hard. She took a shaky breath and she wondered if he was going to hurt her. Possible ways this could go down were running through her head. He didn't look to be the type of guy who was gentle or even sensitive. She just hoped he didn't come at her like a charging animal. She wasn't really sure what to make of a cyborg who wanted to have sex.

Her heart skipped a beat as he bent over to tear at his black boots. He was going to strip down and that only meant one thing. He was really going to have sex with her. She took a step back from him and bumped into the bed with the back of her thighs, leaving her nowhere to go.

His chest was amazing, muscled and well defined. Her gaze flickered over him—a perfect male specimen. Super buff. His skin was beautiful. Not shiny, like some metal, but a dull, lustrous, light silver-gray color. It looked warm and supple. A nice shade that reminded her of some of the new metal engine parts she loved working with, but she was silently freaking out about the whole cyborg thing. Her mind tried frantically to remember any history she knew about cyborgs. She wasn't coming up with much.

Dawn remembered they been designed to for medical purposes, had been grown in labs, similar to the way clones were grown, and then enhanced. Scientists and doctors had used cybernetics to replace missing limbs, failed organs, and they'd managed to map the human brain to help the mentally ill.

Eventually scientists had mated humans with technology enough to produce super-strong men with a projected lifespan of two hundred years. She'd been told that Earth Government had wanted pilots for deep-space-exploration flights to seek out other life and life-sustaining planets, to find new resources. With their new technology and implants, cyborgs were stronger, faster, and supposedly possessed computer-like brains, giving them super intelligence as well. Her father had told her they lacked emotions and were robotic so space madness, which afflicted some human travelers on long space journeys, didn't happen to cyborgs.

They had been flawed though. She had learned that they refused to take orders and had turned on humans. Earth Government had deemed the project a failure and ordered all cyborgs destroyed. There had been

24

rumors that some had escaped before the military could put them to death. Obviously that rumor had been true since one was stripping naked just feet from her.

Her gaze roamed broad shoulders with tattoos that ran from his collarbones, over the top of his shoulders and then disappeared to his back. His biceps were thick masses of muscle that were bigger around than her thighs, maybe even her waist. She swallowed hard, her attention lowering to his pants, which he slowly unfastened. He had ridges of muscle just above his belt. Her heart hammered. He looked too big and too strong for it to even be safe to have sex with someone such as him. If he didn't manage to bruise her up being too rough, then he'd definitely squish her with his weight.

Intense blue eyes watched her from beneath long, curly dark red eyelashes. His luminous skin tone and red hair was shocking enough but as his pants slid down tapered hips she was in for another stunning moment. The gasp she heard came from her own lips as her terrified gaze locked on his sex.

"Oh, hell no." She tried to back up, forgetting she was already against his bed, only to collapse on her ass on his mattress at the sudden motion.

His full lips twisted into a smirk. "You're my slave and you agreed to this." His voice was deeper than normal but in a lower tone that reminded her more of a growl.

Dawn couldn't look away from the cyborg's protruding cock, which was pointing right at her as he kicked out of his leather pants and boots, stepping free of them to remove his socks. He straightened, took a step toward her. She whimpered, shaking her head again.

"You're too thick, too big, and I can't." She never thought she'd be telling a guy he was too big but she'd never seen one built the way the cyborg was either. He wasn't freaky large but that was more than she'd ever seen and she hadn't had sex in two years, four months, and some weeks. Her gaze tore from his generous sex to plead with him with her eyes. "You'll hurt me."

He froze, stared at her, looking seriously annoyed. His eyes narrowed and his expression became grim. Taking a deep breath that expanded his chest further, he growled low in his throat. The animalistic sound made her even more afraid.

"I'll be careful. The last thing I want to do is hurt you."

She so didn't believe him. She inched back on his mattress until her head bumped the wall, telling her she was trapped in the corner with no escape. Her gaze was locked with his and fear turned to outright terror as he took a step toward her and then another, advancing on her the way a predator would, toying with its prey.

"Please," she whispered. "You're seriously the size of two of me and with that..." her gaze flew down to his cock again and then back up. "That's going to hurt me."

His eyes flashed then all expression was wiped away. He stopped at the edge of the bed, staring down at her, not even blinking now. "Open your thighs and let me see you."

"No."

26

That got a reaction from him. Iron frowned. "If you don't want to be hurt then open up and let me see. Don't make me say it again. I can make you do anything I want. We both know I'm much stronger than you but I don't want to have to force you because I'd have to pin you, which might harm you."

She hesitated.

"I want to see if you can take me without pain…or not. Like males, females come in different sizes. If you are as small as you are implying I will see that and know that sex isn't possible between us without harming you. Open your thighs to me and I'll be the judge."

She finally shook her head. "No."

He took another deep breath, drawing her attention to his wide chest again. Then he spun away. He took a few rapid steps to his discarded clothing, bent over to show her a nice, muscular silver-gray ass, then he straightened and turned back to face her. He was gripping his belt.

"What are you going to do with that?" She went from terror to anger. "If you hit me, you better knock me out or I'll kill your ass."

She moved, getting to her feet on his bed. Being taller than him helped him look only slightly less intimidating. She balled her fists, tensing. She'd fight before she submitted to some asshole whipping her.

He watched her a moment before he struck. He moved faster than she thought possible for such a hulking frame. He almost dove at her, going low, not giving her time to react as his hand gripped her ankle. She didn't even have time to scream as he gave a mighty jerk, yanking her legs out from under her. She hit the bed on her back, in shock, before weight crushed her down as the cyborg fell on top of her.

She stared up at his face, unable to even breathe from his weight, feeling crushed into the soft mattress. Hot skin pressed tightly to her cooler flesh. She didn't fight when he jerked her arms above her head. She was too stunned and the panic of not being able to get air into her lungs made her freeze up. When the urge to breathe became unbearable she started to fight.

His weight lifted off her, allowing her the air she needed as she gasped it in. The man pinning her used his hands to brace his upper body, their gazes locking—hers terrified and his grim. She tried to push him but her arms wouldn't come down. She jerked and felt the bite of his belt on her wrists instead. Her wrists were tied together, attached to his headboard.

"Let me go."

He slowly shook his head, lifting off her. "Open your legs now for my inspection."

"Fuck you." She locked her legs together as he moved to sit on the side of the mattress, turning to stare at her legs.

He frowned. "I could force them open but then you'd have bruises."

Glaring at him, feeling afraid at the same time, she hesitated. "When I get free, I'm going to kill your ass."

An eyebrow arched. "Thank you for sharing your plan with me." His voice deepened. "Now open up for my inspection. Resisting me is a waste of your energy and will only harm you."

Gritting her teeth, she drew her knees up to her chest, hesitated, and then twisted her body suddenly and slammed the bastard in his chest. She kicked out hard, and to her shock, actually knocked him off the bed. She watched him disappear off the edge and heard the satisfying sound of him landing on the floor with a grunt.

He came up fast, anger on his features, and then he reached for her with his big hands. Struggling and trying to kick him didn't work for long. The big cyborg grabbed her thighs, pressing them to the bed. He forced her legs open and pinned them down. Dawn screamed in rage. He ignored her to stare at her exposed pussy.

She stared at his face. He frowned and his gaze lifted. "Activate your sex drive now."

"What?"

He sighed. "You're not ready for sex. Activate your sex drive so you are prepared for my cock."

Shock tore through her as his words sank in. She struggled, straining against his hands on her thighs and the belt that kept her arms together over her head but all she did was twist helplessly. She glared at him, letting her anger override her fear.

"I'm not a computer. I can't get turned-on at a command, asshole. Is that how your women are? That's just freaky."

He blinked a few times while he studied her. "I want you wet and ready for me."

"I want you to let me go, you gray bastard. I can't just do that because you tell me to."

His hands jerked away from her, releasing her thighs, which she immediately locked together. He stood up in a fluid motion and stormed across the room. Dawn watched the big man slam a fist into the wall, taking loud, long deep breaths. He stood there with his back to her before he slowly turned to face her again. Rage was etched on his face.

"I demand you prepare your body for me. I control the fate of the younger human you care for so you will do as I say."

She moved on the bed, using her feet to push on the mattress and managed to sit up, her back to the headboard as she tugged uselessly on her bound wrists. The belt was tight on her skin, the weird, stretchy material it was made of dug into her wrists almost painfully. She just stared at the cyborg in shock. He honestly thought she could just flip a mental switch and want him. Were they like that? Sexual desire just something cyborgs could turn on and off in their brains? She swallowed.

"I'm human. I can't just want you because you tell me to. I don't want you and I'm afraid. The only way I'm going to get wet is if I piss myself."

He growled low, a frustrated sound. He bent suddenly to grab his clothes up off the floor. She watched him get dressed in jerky motions. Relief hit her as he stormed out of the room a minute later, leaving her alone. Her heart rate slowed as her fear and anger eased away. She turned her attention to the belt that held her secured to his bed.

"Fuck." She tugged and even managed to bend and twist enough to use her teeth but she couldn't get free.

* * * * *

It was dark in the room. The lights had just gone out and it had scared her when blackness surrounded her. The cyborg's room was too quiet. The reinforced walls kept out all sound. On Vonder Station, the sound of the engines running was always a constant, soothing hum. On the *Star* it was similar to being sealed inside a tomb.

She was curled in a ball on her side, cold, miserable, and scared. Had Iron gone to hurt Cathy? Would the girl pay because Dawn had fought off the man, prevented him from taking her by force? He scared her and she admitted that freely. He was big, alien looking, and not all the way human. She knew cyborgs were mostly human because they got their DNA from human donors but that's where the similarities ended. They were machines under their skin, even if they were flesh and blood ones.

The door opened suddenly, light blinding her as the room flooded with it automatically, telling her that she wasn't alone anymore. She blinked to adjust to the light and turned her head to stare over her shoulder to see what would happen in her living nightmare now. Iron stepped inside the door as it slid closed behind him. His blue gaze locked with hers.

"I'm back."

"I see." She didn't move and kept rolled in a tight ball on his bed with her back to him. He could see her ass but she couldn't help that since she was naked. "Did you hurt Cathy?"

"No. I was doing research."

Why did that scare her? Dawn chewed on her lip, afraid to ask what the hell that meant. She rolled over, facing him, though still tightly balled, hiding her body from his gaze.

He reached for his shirt, slowly removing it to show off his chest again. He stripped out of his pants. He had not put on his boots, had left the room barefoot, so it didn't take him long to undress. Dawn refused to glance down his big body to see if he was turned-on again. She had a sinking feeling that the cyborg was going to take another run at her for sex.

"I just watched a male stimulate his human female's sexual responses." He tilted his head, staring at her. "I learn quickly."

That totally didn't bode well for her and she knew it as she stared at him. "Good for you."

"Good for us." He turned away to walk toward a storage wall. "I know how to prepare you for my cock now." He opened up part of the wall.

"Son of a bitch," she whispered, struggling to sit up. He was aroused, his cock thick, stiff, and protruding straight from his large frame as he turned to face her again. She glanced at that generous endowment and locked her thighs tightly together, feeling her heart rate climb to an accelerated pace.

"Don't do this. You're a cyborg and obviously you have the ability to turn your needs on or off at a thought. Shut it down."

He walked over and dropped a few shirts on the end of the bed. "I can control my body but I have often suffered sexual urges. I own you now so I no longer have to deny myself a basic need."

A chime sounded. It made Dawn jump, not expecting it. The cyborg turned away from her, walking calmly and totally naked to his door. It opened up as he approached, the automatic sensors doing their job. Dawn gasped when she saw two more cyborgs standing there. Their gazes went directly to her and her naked body.

"Fuck," she cursed, jerking her knees up, trying to hide her exposed body to their view. Terror hit her as the two men started to step into the room. That son of a bitch was going to turn her into a ship whore to share with his buddies. "No!"

Iron ignored her to step back. "Bring it in."

A third cyborg suddenly came into view, although he was difficult to see behind the cot he carried. It was an entire framed unit with mattress and rails. There wasn't much room to spare as the men all worked together to put it down flat between the cleansing room area and the end of the bed. Dawn huddled tighter, terrified, watching the three strange cyborgs send looks her way that told her they were interested in her.

"Leave," Iron ordered the men. "Thank you for your assistance."

One of the men hesitated when the other two turned away to leave. The dark-skinned cyborg with black hair and dark eyes remained. "A word, Iron?"

Iron frowned but nodded. Iron crossed his arms over his chest, seemingly oblivious to his naked body or aroused state. He could have been fully dressed by the way he behaved as he waited for the other cyborg to talk.

"I haven't had a female in a very long time. Would you consider either trading her? I will give you use of her body for free for the first month as a bonus. I could make a good profit with her on the ship. Many males would pay a high price for her."

"No!" Dawn shouted. Her terrified look centered on Iron, who met her eyes with a bored expression. "Please don't do this to me. I'm not a sex worker. I haven't had sex in two years. I'll make a deal with you."

Red eyebrows arched. "Aren't you going to offer to fight me again to determine your fate?"

Chapter Three

Hatred for this jerk burned through her. He was being a sarcastic prick at the moment. He held her life in his hands now though. She bit back some choice names she wanted to toss at him. She had to take a deep breath to even speak around her anger and fear.

"I won't fight you again if you make him leave. Please don't trade out to other cyborgs."

He just stared at her, expressionless, as the seconds ticked away. She'd kicked him off the bed. Would this be the way he got back at her? She licked her lips, feeling really dry mouthed from her terror.

"Please don't do this to me. You know I'm afraid of you. I'm sorry if I pissed you off but put yourself in my shoes."

"I would never be as weak as you. I would have fought to the death before I allowed myself to be captured."

She bit back the word "asshole". "Please don't do this to me."

"I will let you decide your own fate." He let his arms drop and moved around the bed, having to brush against the other cyborg to reach her. He leaned down, releasing her wrists with just a few quick motions of his hands. "Do what I say and show me that keeping you with me for my private use is a good investment."

Dawn lunged, grabbed the cover from his bed and jerked the material over her exposed body to hide it from both men's view.

She rubbed her wrists as he backed away from her. She was free. Her gaze jerked to the other cyborg. He was watching her intently, his dark gaze scaring her. Her attention went to Iron, hating him a bit more because she knew whatever he ordered her to do, she'd have to obey or face the consequences by possibly being given to the other male.

"Stand up and go lie flat on your back on the cot."

Hot tears burned the back of her eyes as she got to her feet. Her hands fisted the cover, tearing if off the bed to clutch it to her chest, hiding as much of bared body as possible. She put her chin up, trying to conceal how vulnerable and embarrassed she was over being so exposed. She moved to the cot, only hesitating for a second while she adjusted the cover before she lay down flat on her back. She held really still, waiting to see what he had in store for her.

"I want your hands above your head. Grip the bar of the frame with your palms up, fingers curled around the metal."

It was hard to let go of the material, knowing he could just jerk it off to expose her to the other man but she released the cover and reached up. One day, if she survived this, he'd let his guard down and she'd get even with him for all of this, she silently swore. The metal was cold as her fingers curled around it. Iron grabbed the shirts he had dumped on the bed and approached her. He didn't look at her or meet her eyes as he bent. She heard material tear and didn't jerk away from his touch as he used the arms of one of his shirts to bind her wrists to the bar above her head. The material wrapped over her fingers, securing them in place firmly. His gaze met hers and she saw amusement flicker in his eyes.

Oh yeah, she swore to herself silently, *the first chance I get, I am going to kill you.* She was humiliated, terrified, and he was enjoying it, not even bothering to hide it from her as he continued to stare at her. He finally lowered his gaze to her covered legs.

"Spread your legs open wide. I want your feet flat on the frame just under your ass and your knees over the edge of each side."

She closed her eyes to hide the tears that surfaced. It was pure hell as she was forced to submit to his demands. She was terrified that he was lying to her as she spread her thighs, wiggling so that when her legs slid out from under the material it stayed bunched in the center. She put her feet on the cold metal sides of the cot, grateful the cover was hiding her pussy, which would have been exposed to his view as her knees dropped all the way open. If he let that other cyborg rape her after she complied... She pushed that thought away, not even wanting to deal with that horror.

Material brushing against her knee made her jerk but she only tensed, not fighting him or trying to get away. Her eyes opened when the material tightened around her thigh. She looked down to see what he was doing to her. Shock tore through her as she realized he was binding her legs open by using a shirt to tie her in place. He was at least careful to keep her vital girl parts covered.

He straightened fully and then just stepped over her and the cot to reach the other side. He crouched there, another shirt in his hand as he set to work on her other leg, tying to the frame. Movement in her peripheral vision made her attention jerk away from Iron and what he was doing. The other cyborg stepped closer, his gaze locked on her body.

"I want to see all of her. She's small."

"I know," Iron tied off the shirt and stood. "It was expected that she be smaller framed than our women. They made us much larger than standard humans."

"I've done human females. I meant she is too thin. In order for her to survive long she needs to gain mass."

They thought she was too thin? Dawn gritted her teeth. She not only was terrified and humiliated by being totally vulnerable in the worst way a woman could be, her legs tied open while she was naked under a thin cover that barely hid her nudity, but they were discussing her as if she were a piece of furniture not to their liking. She hoped they weren't interested in her enough to want her though, on second thought.

"Leave," Iron said softly.

The other cyborg frowned. "I'm willing to give you whatever you want for her."

Iron's head snapped up, his eyes narrowed and his expression turned ice cold. "I said leave now or I'll remove you. The female and I agreed to the terms and she is following them by obeying my commands. I ordered you to leave. Consider the viewing of her body as a gift. That's all you're going to get."

The other male's features tightened but he spun away and left the room. Dawn's body relaxed slightly now that the tense moment was over. For a second she thought they'd go to blows and she was on a cot between them. That wouldn't have been good at all. Her gaze turned to Iron. He was already watching her.

"Try to remain relaxed."

She opened her mouth, not sure how to respond to that but he moved then, straddling the cot below her. Her gaze followed him as he sat just a few feet from where her legs were tied open. Big hands gripped the cover, and with one jerk, he bared her entire body to his view. He dropped the cover onto the floor next to the cot. He lowered his gaze to stare with concentration at her pussy.

"Please don't—"

"Silence." His intense look rose to meet hers. "I will activate your sex drive for you and then I will carefully possess your body. I don't wish you harm."

He is going to activate my sex drive? Who talks like that? She frowned but then reminded herself he was a cyborg. Obviously they weren't romantic in any way imaginable. She tried to wiggle away as his warm hand wrapped around her inner thigh and his fingers curled close to her sex but she was tied down too tightly to be able to move away.

"Wait a second. I think we should talk about this. I—"

He growled low in his throat, the sound scary. "I said be silent. You agreed to be my slave." His eyes narrowed dangerously. "This is not a time for you to be human with your wasted emotions." He hesitated. "They are no concern to me. I want sex and I am willing to activate you to do it but if you anger me our joint pleasure will no longer be a goal of mine."

Her mouth opened and slammed closed. She took a breath as anger flooded her. "Like I'm going to enjoy this no matter how it goes down. Right.

Let me clue you in, cyborg. Unless you vibrate and are shaped like my favorite sex toy, there isn't going to be any joint pleasure."

The hand on her thigh tightened. "You're comparing me to a sex toy?"

Had she insulted him?

"Do you have a sex droid model? We have stolen a few shipments of them so I'm aware of what they are and their functions." His tone lowered to a gravelly tone. "You compare me to one of those brainless robots? They say about forty phrases and you have to position them to move the way you want them to before activating them." He glared at her. "They are very limited at even that." He paused. "You said you hadn't had sex in two years. I am starting to understand why human males won't touch you. You are a very disagreeable female. I can assure you I am nothing like a sex droid."

"Tried one, did you? You sound like you know a lot about them. Was it your girlfriend?" Damn, she regretted saying that as soon as the words were out of her mouth. Sometimes she said things before her brain caught up and she was always flip with her remarks, especially when angry.

He glared at her. She glared back. So far he hadn't hurt her but she figured if she didn't get control of her temper that would change fast. She wondered if she'd already pushed him too far.

"Sex droids may have limited speech but at least they don't talk offensively. Has anyone ever told you that you have a foul mouth for a female?"

"If you wanted someone with polite conversational skills you should have kidnapped a diplomat. I'm a mechanic who grew up around men. I had to work so I never attended charm school."

He leaned forward as his attention returned to her exposed pussy. She tensed as his hand left her thigh and both his hands reached between them. She jerked as his thumbs spread her farther apart, opening her sex lips wide. He ignored her struggles while he shifted his big body back to lower his face until his hot breath fanned her exposed pussy.

"Do you know what I'm going to enjoy more than fucking you?" He didn't wait for an answer. "The knowledge that you can resist me but you can't win. That is punishment enough for your insults."

"Fuck you, cyborg. Go ahead and try to activate me. I did agree to this and I keep my word so let's get this over with. Just do what you want to my body but you better not hurt me."

He growled a second before shock tore through her as his mouth closed over her clit. It was hot and wet, shocking her. He hesitated only a second before he tested the flesh against his tongue by licking her. She jerked hard in her restraints, trying to get away, but she couldn't. He'd tied her legs too securely for her to move away from his seeking mouth.

Dawn closed her eyes tightly as she turned her head, trying not to feel anything as his tongue lapped at her clit. It was a shocking sensation and worse, it was starting to feel good, pleasurable in a raw way. She realized that her tense body made it worse, enhancing the sensation even more so she forced herself to relax. Some of the pleasure eased back but it was still there.

His mouth and tongue toyed with her clit, drawing her body toward response. Her nipples tightened in and her belly quivered along with her vaginal walls. A moan started to build so she clenched her teeth together. She'd rather die than let the bastard hear how he was turning her on.

She arched her back, lifting it from the mattress but it didn't her get her farther away from that mouth. If anything it pressed her pussy tighter against his face. She jerked back down and turned her head the other way as her hands gripped the metal in a white-knuckled hold.

He growled against her clit, sending vibrations through the oversensitive, hardening flesh. A small whimper came from her throat, though she hadn't meant to make it. Breathing was getting difficult as she took choppy breaths, gasping air into her lungs when she realized she'd been holding her breath. He sucked on her, licked at her harder, with more pressure, increasing the speed of his tongue, rubbing up and down against the sensitive nub.

She was going to come. She tried to imagine a dead body, the time the sewage line had burst on the space station and she'd literally had to clean up shit for a week but not even her worst memories could mute her pleasure. Dawn knew she couldn't fight her body and the jackass had been right. He was totally in control of her body now. Her body tensed in anticipation a few seconds before rapture tore through her as the climax hit. She cried out, unable to stop the sound that passed her lips.

The hot mouth tore away from her. She sagged in relief, her pussy clenching and twitching from her release, and she realized she was panting as if she'd gone jogging as the pleasure-induced haze started to clear.

A thick finger slowly pushed inside her pussy, unexpected. Her eyes flew open and she couldn't look away from the man between her spread thighs. His full lips curved into a smirk of satisfaction as he watched her through hooded eyes.

"You're prepared for me." He withdrew his finger from her body. "Now you're going to take me."

He shifted on the cot, his hands coming down next to her chest to grip the edges of the bed frame. She just stared up at him in mute shock as he stretched out over her, keeping his weight off her while he positioned his body. He slowly lowered over her. She gasped as his hard cock pressed against her wet pussy and then, with a small hip adjustment on his part, he came down on her, letting gravity work with him to push into her.

She threw her head back as his thick, rigid cock breached her pussy. Her vagina stretched to accommodate the big cyborg, her treacherous body soaked to help ease him inside her. He kept pushing his cock into her, making her body take more and more of him, until he settled snuggly on top of her.

She'd never been so full in her life as she was at that moment. His cock was thick, hard, and just...big. Her pussy was wrapped tight around him, almost to the point of pain. He didn't move on her, just took slow, deep breaths. She opened her eyes, wondering why he was frozen there over her. She couldn't stop him, had agreed to this and couldn't fight back even if she hadn't, so why wasn't he just fucking her already?

Dawn couldn't help but notice his eyes were beautiful up close. They were a dark blue with flecks of a lighter shade of blue. Their faces were almost nose-to-nose. He had lowered his head enough to level them out some, though he was quite a bit taller than her. He was staring into her eyes and she couldn't look away. He took another slow, deep breath, making his chest crush down on hers just enough to make her aware that if his arms weren't bracing his upper-body weight, she wouldn't be able to breathe.

"Should I fuck you like one of those droids?"

Speechless, she just stared at him.

He slowly withdrew almost totally out of her body and then pushed back in. She closed her eyes at the wonderful sensation. He was so thick that she could feel him hitting every nerve ending she had. She was turned-on and the sensations were really good, though she'd rather die than admit it to him.

He lowered his face to the side of her neck. His breath was hot, fanning her skin, tickling a little before he froze on her again. "I'm not a sex droid. They don't kiss or adjust their movements to the little gasps and moans you make. I do all that."

His lips whispered across her skin under her ear, causing her to shiver in the good way, her breasts puckering as his hot skin slid against them. Inside her, his cock throbbed, buried deep, and it was a pleasurable sensation. His tongue rasped against her earlobe before teeth gently nipped. She turned her head more, giving him freer access.

"Tell me you want me," he murmured as he scattered teasing little kisses and nips over the side of her neck. "Do you want me fast and hard or slow, with me almost removing my cock from you, to drive in deep again, over and over?"

Her pussy clenched in response, her back arching. She wasn't in control anymore and didn't even want to be. Raw lust flared in her and as she turned her head, she forced him to pull back so she could look into his eyes as she made a decision.

"Fast and hard but I need my clit stimulated."

If he was surprised at her answer, he hid it well. He nodded and shifted a little, adjusting the angle of his cock so he pressed against her exposed clit. He started to move then, thrust into her fast, pulled back fast, and drove forward so their skin slapped together.

Dawn watched his face, experiencing rapture as her body responded to the overload of sensations his pounding cock gave her. He didn't ease up on her clit, careful that every motion he made in and out of her body rubbed against her swollen bud, the wetness from her soaking them both, making them a well-oiled sex machine, together. She knew she was close, knew he was close when she saw his eyes close, his jaw clench. Sweat beaded his brow. He was fighting the urge to come, she knew it, and took satisfaction that she wasn't the only one gripped by the passion that flared between them.

Giving in to the pleasure, she let herself come. The climax tore through her and a cry came from her parted lips. She could feel him blasting his release inside her, while hot jets of semen filled her, felt good to her. She'd never come so hard in her life, she realized seconds later when the haze of sheer bliss faded enough to take in the fact that he was still buried balls-deep in her pussy and she was pressed tight against him.

Iron's eyes opened. "I'm better than a sex droid, aren't I?"

She was tempted to say no, to flat out lie, but then she saw a hint of something in his eyes. She was good at reading people, had to be with all the women she'd dealt with over the years that she'd had to try to keep sane on a small space station. She saw loneliness in his beautiful gaze, even a hint of insecurity, and a possible need for someone to boost his ego. Maybe he wasn't such a cold bastard after all.

"You're much better."

His body relaxed and his lips curved upward just slightly.

"This will work between us."

Dawn licked her lips. "If you think it's going to be that easy, think again."

Iron's smile died. "You're going to be difficult for me?"

She smiled. "You have no idea."

Chapter Four

Dawn paced the small quarters, feeling anger. Where was Iron? She looked at the clock on the wall. Eight hours had passed since he'd brought her breakfast, leaving again after spending only few minutes in the room. She was hungry and he'd deactivated the inner door panel so she couldn't jimmy the control pad to escape. She really wished that Cathy hadn't told him that she had the skill to open any door.

She'd had last night and all day to think. There hadn't been anything else to do but deal with her thoughts and she had enjoyed that foam cleansing unit he had. It beat rubbing gel on her skin and just letting it air dry. The foam sprayed her naked body, fizzed in a pleasant way while it cleaned her until it melted like water to drip down her body. She'd been refreshed afterward. The cyborg even had thick, soft towels to dry with. The *Star* was a luxury class-A starship which, hands down, was better than the space station she lived on.

She was stuck with Iron until she could find a way to escape. That could take some time, she knew, and that meant she could either pout or make the best of her situation. Iron was great in bed, that was a plus, and she wasn't going to be spare parts for any of his friends.

Dawn admitted to being a realist. She'd had to become one in her lifetime, never having a privileged life, to help support her large family from the time she was twelve when she'd ditched school to work with her father fixing hovercrafts in the shop he owned. She'd enjoyed the work, liked to

47

get her hands dirty, and she was more about life lessons than schoolbooks any day.

Her father, Sean McShay, hadn't been a big man but he'd been tough and had swiftly kicked the ass of any boy who looked twice at any of his six daughters. She'd had to move off a planet to get laid the first time when she was twenty. Her first post had been on a garbage crawler, a big beast of a ship that hauled trash from Earth to dispose of it on Jupiter's largest moon, Ganymede. While onboard she'd had to watch her back with the mostly male crew, sticking with Mack Thomas who didn't share what was his, protected her, and kept other men from even thinking about touching her. He'd taught her about sex, how to fight to defend herself and she'd fallen head over heels in love with him.

That seemed like a lifetime ago. Bitterness still burned in her heart when she thought of Mack. For two years they'd been lovers and in all that time he'd never mentioned the wife or five kids he had back on Earth until they were days from returning home. He'd wanted to keep her on the side, continue their relationship when he came back for duty with her. Worse, he'd broken her young, foolish heart. She'd learned to never let her emotions get involved again.

She'd changed posts then and had taken a job for Earth Government to avoid Mack. She'd heard about the Arian Nine project, wanted on board the Vonder Station and had hired on while it was still in space dock being built. She'd cut her teeth as a mechanic on space stations there under the careful watch of four female mechanics who had taught her everything she needed to know. Eight years ago the Vonder had been put into orbit around Arian Nine and Dawn had been assigned as the lead mechanic. It was her baby to keep it and the planet's machines going. It was also a totally female crew, her dream place to be, and it kept her from making the same mistake twice. No men meant there was no one to fall in love with.

The times she'd hooked up with guys on leave had left her unsatisfied. She'd used men for sex and had climbed out of their beds the second the panting ended. It had been decent sex sometimes but nothing close to the quickie she'd shared with Iron the night before. She took a deep breath. Maybe it was the bondage thing. *Maybe I'm twisted that way and that's why I got so turned on.* Those thoughts comforted her because the sex with the big cyborg had been the best she'd ever had.

The door suddenly opened and Iron stepped in carrying a tray of food. Her stomach grumbled loudly at the smell. She lunged forward and just tore it from his hands. She saw surprise raise his eyebrows but she didn't care. She turned to present her back to him as she stormed for the bed.

"If you're going to own a person, you should remember to feed them. I've been starving, damn it." She set down the tray and collapsed on the bed next to it and scanned the food. "Thank God you bastards eat meat. I was afraid I'd get more bread like you brought me this morning."

"You are welcome," Iron growled. "Hello to you. My work shift was fine. Thank you for asking."

Popping a piece of stripped meat into her mouth, Dawn turned her head. Iron stood leaning against the door with his arms crossed over his chest. The annoyed expression on his face amused her a little. She knew she was being rude but damn, the man should feed her if he was going to lock her up. She chewed, savoring the good steak flavor and then swallowed.

"Feed me more often if you want me polite."

"I express my regret. I didn't mean to be gone for so long."

She was surprised he'd apologize. She hesitated. "Have you ever owned someone before?"

"No. You are the first."

"I see." She really didn't. "So I take it humans are possessions to your kind?"

"We were possessions on Earth so it is fitting, now that we are free, that we apply your laws to you."

"Ah." She nodded. "I'm a revenge slave. Great. I wasn't responsible for that shit. It's really hard to find out much about that part of our history but I know you were mistreated. I didn't do it though."

"Mistreated?" His tone lowered in anger. "We were used, ordered around like robots and when we said no to their demands, they slated us for execution."

Dawn swallowed another bite, eating quickly. "That was messed up. Don't take it out on me though, okay?" She shifted her gaze to his hair, fascinated with how red and bright it was. "Take your hair out of the braid."

"Why?"

"I want to see it. Are you part Irish or Scottish?" She touched her hair. "I get my red hair and green eyes from my father. He's pure Irish, one of the remaining last few whose bloodlines weren't mixed. He met my mother though and fell in love so his family disowned him. They were purists who believed you should stick to your own kind and she wasn't a hundred-percent Irish. Her mother was French."

"I have no idea what kind of heritage my donors were who gave up their DNA for my creation." He paused. "Nor do I care. I rarely unbind my hair other than to free it every day when I get clean. I then braid it again. I like to keep it under control."

"Well, take it down and show me before you get clean. You just got off work and you didn't use the foam cleansing unit this morning when you brought me breakfast so do it now."

"I did cleanse but not here. I keep another room down the hall." He paused. "Stop giving me orders."

"Why do you have another room? I thought this one was yours."

"It is but I decided to take one of the empty quarters for sleeping and cleansing."

"I thought you were working last night and then again today." Her mind went into overdrive. "You didn't just pull two full shifts, did you?"

"I slept down the hallway."

"I see." Her temper flared. "I'm good enough to fuck once but I'm not good enough to sleep with? This room is like a tomb. I froze my ass off last night since that thin cover doesn't do shit and you're telling me I could have used your body heat to stay warm? Nice."

"The room temperature isn't to your liking?" He pushed away from the wall. "Why didn't you say something?"

"Would you have cared?"

His frown was instant. "What is your preference for the temperature? I'll set the control to that."

She was surprised that he'd care if she was chilled in his room and a little touched that he was willing to adjust the controls to her specification. She told him what she preferred. He nodded, cocked his head, and closed his eyes. In seconds his blue eyes opened back up.

"Done."

She swallowed her surprise. "You just remote accessed the room controls with your mind?"

"Yes. With your talent for opening doors, I assumed you could do other things so I have deactivated everything in the room but basic things like the foam cleanser and the lighting controls. All other functions are remotely controlled by me."

She bit her lip and then stood, inched closer to him. She hated to admit it even to herself but she was fascinated. "What do you have under your skin?"

Iron's eyes narrowed as he stared down at her. "Why do you want to know? Are you seeking weaknesses to attack?"

"Man, are you paranoid. No. I'm a mechanic. What are you running under your skin?"

He paused, studying her carefully. "I have enhancements."

"I get that." She rolled her eyes and stopped feet from him to stare up into his handsome features. He was good looking. "What kind?"

"I have several chips embedded in my brain that were implanted to help me control my body functions and a processor to calculate and store information." He paused. "I have a limited range for sending and receiving signals but that ability was given to me so I could pilot a shuttle faster."

"Shit. You can access everything aboard a shuttle without moving to different stations, can't you?"

"Yes. I was one of the first prototypes in the pilot program on Earth."

Shock tore through her. "That's impossible." Her gaze swept over him from head to foot. He looked maybe thirty-eight years old, tops. Closer to thirty-five, actually. "You'd be old if that were true."

"Just my donors were human. Cyborgs were designed to age slower. I have no reason to lie. I was a pilot prototype on Earth."

"Shit!" She took a step back from him. "That means you're as old as my father."

He shrugged. "What is the relevance?"

"We had sex." She made a face. "I did someone my father's age. That's just wrong."

A spark of some emotion flashed in his eyes. "I bet I do not look like your father."

Her gaze slowly went over him this time, taking in his broad shoulders, the massive leather-clad, thick biceps, his firm, flat stomach, his tapered hips, and down his thick, muscular thighs. "No. You sure don't. Even in my father's prime he wasn't built like you. He's small and wiry."

"Is he still alive then?"

"Yeah. My folks live on Earth. I go visit them every time I'm off duty and take the shuttle to Earth. I paid for some medical enhancements for

53

them so they are in decent shape for their age but damn..." She moved closer to him, her attention locked on his body still. "For an old guy, you have it going on."

"What does that mean?"

She looked up into his face. The sex between them had been great and she was curious. "Take off your clothes. I can totally mind-wash the thought of how old you are when I see you naked. You look my age and you've got the best body I've ever seen."

His eyebrows rose. "What did you say?"

"I said take off your clothes. I'm your sex slave, right? It's damn hard to have sex if you're dressed." She reached for her jumpsuit, opening it up. "I spent two years alone with a vibrator I could barely use. Do you know how difficult it is to find time alone with a bunch of women clambering all over a space station? Forget doing it in my bunk. The crew was all together in bunks long hallway. If you sneezed everyone heard it within twenty feet down on either side. The only real offers of sex I got were from a few other women I work on the station with but I don't swing that way. I'm here, you're here, and it was great last time so let's go for it."

He didn't move, just stared at her, looking a little stunned. Dawn stripped naked and moved toward him. "Activate your sex drive. You can do that, right? Get hard for me, big guy. We're here, I'm a prisoner, and I've spent the day bored as shit. You can at least fuck me and make it up to me."

He opened his mouth and then slammed it closed. His dark blue eyes narrowed. "You're ordering me to have sex with you? You're *my* slave."

She grinned and reached for the front of his pants to unfasten his belt, amused when he kept his arms crossed over his chest, unmoving. She'd always loved a challenge.

"You'll learn some things about me if you plan on keeping me locked in your room." She let his belt hit the floor and started to open his pants. She saw his reaction as his cock started to fill out under her hands, the outline of thickening male flesh obvious to the eye. "I have a temper. I also have a twisted sense of humor. Maybe it's the Irish in me but I tend switch my moods fast. Piss me off, I'll make you wish you hadn't but if you get me in a good mood I'm pretty easy going." She jerked his pants down his hips, her thumbs hooking his black briefs, baring his beautiful skin. She was getting used to the soft silver color. She tugged down until his thick and impressively sized cock sprang free. "I also am sex starved. I think I've hit my sexual prime and if you're going to make me a sex slave then I'm going to take advantage of the situation."

Iron sucked in air loudly as Dawn released his pants and wrapped one of her hands around his cock. He was so thick that her index finger and thumb couldn't touch. Her other hand wiggled between his body and his pants, trapped at his thighs, to cup his balls. They were hairless, heavy, and filled her palm. She smiled, looking up into his face.

"You've got balls, I'll say that about you." She massaged them gently to make a point. "Now I'll make a deal with you."

His jaw clenched. "I see. You want to negotiate for sex. I won't give you freedom." His hand snaked out, grabbing both of her wrists to jerk her hands from his body. "I won't be manipulated that way. If I want to fuck you, I'll turn you around, bend you over, and take you."

55

The idea of him doing that had Dawn's nipples hardening. She wasn't some shrinking violet. She was a mechanic, tough, and she liked her sex a little rough. Not bruising, but damn, it turned her on, remembering him fucking her the night before, his powerful body over hers. He'd been careful to not hurt her, though he could have.

"Promises, promises," she muttered, knowing she was playing a dangerous game with the cyborg. He wasn't really a man, nothing similar to anything she'd ever dealt with. This wasn't some guy she was desperate and lonely enough to pick up in a bar on Earth. She'd done that a few times over the years but short-term sex was never satisfying and she always ran the risk of getting some guy who wouldn't care if she got off or not. "I wasn't going to ask for my freedom."

"What do you want from me to have sex?"

Licking her lips, Dawn swallowed as a blush warmed her cheeks. For as outgoing as she was, no matter how tough she tried to project herself, she was still a bit shy with men, concerning sex. She'd never been exposed to that many of them for longer than a night at a time while on leave.

"I want you to do to me what you did last night when you went down on me. I liked that a hell of a lot."

He stared at her. Dawn wanted to curse. He was gripping her wrists, she was naked, his pants were pushed down to his thighs, and his cock was pointing straight out between them. Long seconds ticked by.

"Is this a trick?"

"Man, you are paranoid." She relaxed. "I really loved what you did to me. Can you do it again? If you do, you can fuck me any way you want to."

His cock twitched, waving a little as if it were a thick, rigid flag. "Yes."

"So you'll do that to me again?"

His hands released her wrists. "Get on the bed."

She hesitated. "Which one? You have yours and that cot you leaned against the wall."

He toed off his boots. "Get on my bed unless you want me to tie you down again to the cot."

She turned and walked to his bed. Her heart pounded. She wondered if she'd get as turned-on while not tied down as she had last night. She wanted to find out. She stretched out on his bed, rolling onto her back, and watched as Iron stripped out of all of his clothes. The sight of his beautiful body was one she was starting to appreciate. He was built similar to a bodybuilder and that shade of silver with his blue eyes was striking, kind of sexy, and as he took a step toward her, she decided Iron was definitely eye candy.

He hesitated at the edge of the bed. "Knees up and spread for me."

Dawn moved, lifting her legs and gripped her ankles as she spread her thighs wide open. Heat warmed her cheeks but she wanted this, wanted him, and knew how good it would feel from the last time. Men had done this to her a few times but it hadn't been as good, not even close, to what Iron could do with that mouth of his.

She met his gaze as he shifted onto the bed, going to his hands and knees at the end of the bed, the mattress dipping with his weight. They stared at each other as she licked her lips.

"Thanks."

A dark red brow arched. "For what?"

"Doing this. I know you could have said no."

He hesitated. "I enjoy your taste and the way you respond to me. It made me ache to be inside you. I am looking forward to the experience again."

She held her breath as he lowered his face, his braid sliding over a broad shoulder to land in one long, thick rope over her leg. She shifted her hand from her ankle to touch his tightly bound hair, her fingers testing the soft texture. He followed her focus as he watched her stroke his hair.

"I want you to unbraid your hair."

"Now?"

She hesitated. "After."

"If you are interested in long hair, why do you have yours cut at your shoulders?"

"Have you ever climbed inside an oxygen generator to replace the gears or change the filters?" She tried to not laugh at his puzzled expression. "Yeah. I have to climb inside to get to them. It's super tight in there but it beats taking the whole assembly apart. If I had long hair, I'd have to pin it tight to my head to not get it caught. I'm a mechanic, Iron. I probably should keep it shorter than it is now but sometimes it's the only feminine thing I have left. You've seen my work outfits. I can't wear jewelry. Make-up is a waste of time and the only thing I'd attract is other women, which isn't something I'd like to do."

He frowned. "Your job sounds dangerous."

"Only if someone were to turn on the fans while I'm in there. It wouldn't happen to me twice, I can tell you that. I'd be chopped and diced in seconds."

"Why did you take a dangerous job? You're a woman. Most of the mechanics I have met are male."

"My father is a mechanic. Every weekend since I was four years old he took some of us kids to work with him to give my mother a break from all of us. I was working on hovercrafts about the time I learned how to read. It's something I know and I'm good at it." She paused. "And there's mega money."

Iron's face lowered and Dawn shut up. She closed her eyes as his warm breath fanned her pussy. Her nipples tightened into hard pebbles and her vaginal walls clenched. Anticipation made her breathe a little faster and her heart rate accelerated. She really wanted him to lick her within an inch of her life again.

Thick fingers spread her tender folds as he exposed her clit and opened her up to his view. "You are so pink."

Dawn opened her eyes, looking down her body at his handsome face hovering between her thighs. "You sound surprised."

His gaze lifted to meet hers. "We are gray." His focus went back to her sex.

"Haven't you ever slept with a human besides me?"

He shook his head. "No. Just cyborg women. I was offered the opportunity a few times while on Earth, to have sex with some of my trainers or guards but I was angry at the time, not wanting to be further used by the humans who had created me."

His thumb brushed over her slit, hesitating there and then let the pad of it play with her inner lips to the entrance. "Cyborg women tend to be white here but you are so pink and so small. Did I hurt you at all when I was inside you? It wasn't my intention."

"You felt really good," she admitted softly. "I thought you'd hurt me but you were surprisingly gentle."

He looked back up at her, his eye narrowing. "You expected me to be like a sex droid." His lips tightened into a line. "I'm not."

"I was pissed. I say a lot of stupid things when I'm mad or scared. I was actually both. I don't really think you're a robot."

He moved suddenly, his mouth opening and his tongue came out to brush against her clit. He didn't look away from her eyes, locking gazes with her as he licked again, then again, lapping at her.

Dawn released his braid and gripped her ankle again to keep her legs wide-open and her knees locked near her shoulders. His tongue was a little raspy over her sensitive bud, at first bringing her a good sensation but then he applied more pressure with every flick of his tongue, pushing the hood of her clit up as it hardened with need. The pleasure intensified into raw rapture. She had to close her eyes to break eye contact with him.

Her back arched and moans burst from her. "Oh God, Iron," she panted. "Do that sucking thing. Please?"

His lips wrapped around her swollen clit, sealing over it, and he pressed his face tighter between her thighs as he started to gently suck, his tongue pressed tightly to her bud while he started to furiously rub it against her.

She had to let go of her ankles. She managed to keep her thighs spread, though the urge to slam them closed was there. Her feet ended up somewhere on his warm back as her fingers clawed at the edges of the bed. Her back arched as she bucked her hips, his hands trying to hold her ass to the bed so she didn't get away from that wonderful mouth of his, working her hard now. It built inside her, that sheer bliss and an almost painful need. Her pussy ached to be filled, a warmth spreading down there, knowing she was probably soaked with her need to be fucked, to find release, and her cries were getting louder. She needed to come.

She couldn't take it anymore, it was rapture turning to pain but then Iron moved his thumb, pushed it inside her pussy, and it sent her over the edge. Dawn yelled out Iron's name as she came, the climax tearing through her body as spasms squeezed around his thumb buried inside her. He groaned against her clit and she cried out his name again, trying to twist her hips out of his hold, unable to take more. The pleasure was turning to pain but then he released her clit and removed his thumb from her, letting her go with his mouth. Dawn went limp.

"Oh God," she panted. "You can do that to me any time you want."

"I'll tie you down next time," his voice was raspy, rough, and a little harsh as he spoke. "You are little but you move a lot."

Forcing her eyes open, Dawn looked down at him. "Give me a minute and then it's your turn."

He pushed up to his hands and knees. "Now." He reached for her, gripping her hips, and easily rolled her over.

Dawn found herself face down in seconds, flat on her stomach, and then his hands gripped her hips, lifting her to her knees so her ass was in the air and her face was on the mattress. She grabbed at the bedding to brace, knowing what was coming as the thick crown of his cock brushed the crack of her ass, slid down to the wetness of her release, and slid through it to brush her oversensitive clit before sliding upward, spreading her cream on him to coat his broad crown well.

"Fuck me," she said softly, spreading her thighs a few inches apart.

"Crawl more toward the wall," he ordered her.

She lifted her head and pushed up with her arms to get her chest off the mattress. She crawled to the headboard and gripped it with both hands. When she looked over her shoulder it was to watch Iron inch closer, his cock looking much darker than his lighter skin shade. His cock looked rock hard, bigger than ever, and she could tell he was really turned-on.

"Ease into me. You're big. Once I get adjusted you can fuck me as hard or as fast as you want."

He didn't speak, agreed to nothing, but then he was against her again, his cock head pressing her slit, hesitating there as his hand gripped her hip to hold her steady. He reached up to put his other hand flat on the wall to brace. She looked up at his hand and then he pushed into her.

Dawn gripped the headboard as Iron slowly entered her, stretching her, forcing her to take all of him in one fluid movement until his hips were pressed against her ass. He stopped there, buried deep, making her feel

62

how hard he was, how he filled her pussy snugly, and she could have taken his pulse, the way she could feel his shaft throbbing.

"Tell me if I hurt you," he almost whispered. "You make me feel very pleased."

He started to move then, pulling out torturously slowly and then pressing back in deep. Dawn let her head drop and pushed back slowly, finding his rhythm and meeting it, using her hold on the headboard to brace as well as for leverage. The pace increased and so did the frenzy she experienced to come again. He was pure ecstasy and heaven inside her, making her feel more rapture than she ever had. He moved even faster and the sensation became almost painful, it was that good. Dawn was hovering on climax, so close, and then his hand slid from her hip to her lower stomach until his fingers curved around her mound. Two fingers pressed against her clit, the motion of them fucking rubbed her just right, and that was it for Dawn. She screamed out, her pussy clamping down on his hammering cock, and bliss gripped her so strongly she nearly passed out.

Iron groaned and pushed hard against her ass, his fingers locking on her clit and holding her still suddenly as he slowed his movements to a tight, jerking motion while he came. He shook, holding their bodies locked together at the hips while he jetted his release inside her, blasting her deep with hot semen until he emptied everything he had to give.

"Okay," Dawn had to fight the urge to collapse on the bed since she was trapped between the big man behind her and the headboard. He was still inside her body so she just released the headboard and straightened up on her knees, leaning back into his big body. "We're going to do this a lot."

His stomach muscles, pressed against her back, tightened and the arm that was still braced on the wall, stretched out in front of her over her shoulder, flexed visibly.

"Are we?" Anger sounded in his tone. "You're my slave. You will do what I say and I will decide how often we have sex."

Dawn smiled. She reached back and cupped his muscular ass as her fingers gripped firm flesh. "Yeah. Tell yourself that, Mr. Control Freak, but if I want you, I'm going to have you." She lifted her chin as she turned her head to look up into his face. She had to bite back a laugh at his shocked expression. "You own me right now, correct? Well, that means we're together for a while. If you own me then I own your ass right back." She squeezed that ass before releasing it. "So we'll make the best of it."

His lips parted. He said nothing though. Just pressed his lips tightly together and some emotion she couldn't read flashed in his eyes. "You can't own me the way I own you."

Dawn closed her eyes, letting more of her body relax as she leaned into his body, knowing he was big enough to support her. "We'll see."

He released her, eased out of her body and climbed off the bed.

Chapter Five

"Where are you going?"

Iron paused, gripping his pants as he turned his head to glare at Dawn. "I am going to sleep in my temporary quarters."

Hurt hit Dawn as she scrambled off the bed and anger closely followed. "So that's how it's going to be? You sleep somewhere else, keep me locked in here going nuts with boredom until you decide to feed me or fuck me?"

"I will agree to get you an entertainment unit. I do not want you to be bored or put you at risk of getting deep space sickness by getting cabin fever."

"Nice." Her anger burned. "So this is how it's really going to be? Is that what you're telling me?"

He was watching her but the only expression he revealed was a frown as he slowly dressed, covering up his muscular frame in the dull black, leather uniform he wore. "Is there a problem?"

"Yes, there's a problem." She stormed up to him, ignoring the fact that she was naked. He'd seen it all so she wasn't about to take the time to cover up. "I'm not some space hooker so don't treat me like one. I take care of my holo PF better than this."

"Holo PF? What is that?"

She hesitated. "I can't have a real pet on the Vonder so I have a holographic pet friend. He's a dog I named Skipper. I know he's just a program but I spend time with him, talk to him, and he isn't even real." She paused. "I am."

"What do you want?"

"Well, that's a loaded question. Released would be nice but I know that isn't going to happen. To start with, you can move your butt back in here and sleep with me."

His lips pressed together and his nostrils flared as he took a deep breath. "No."

"No? I'm good enough to fuck but not to live with? You'll get close and personal with me while we're physical but you won't let me sleep with you?"

"Exactly."

Dawn shoved her hands out and pushed on his hard chest, surprising him enough that he stumbled back a step. She spun on her heel and walked a few feet away to put space between them before she faced him again.

"Fine. You want to play it this way? That was the last damn time you fuck me, pal. Until you change your mind and treat me with some respect and like something more than a piece of ass, you aren't touching me."

Iron crossed his arms over his chest. "You've agreed to be my slave."

"Slave, yes. Hooker? No. People live with their pets, let them sleep with them, spend time with them, and talk to them. I should rate higher than pet status." She ran to the door, blocking his exit. She reached out and gripped the sides of the doorframe. "You're not leaving until we work this out. I refuse to sit in here fuming until tomorrow morning."

"You don't issue demands. You're the slave."

"Then be a better slave owner," she shot back. "And then I wouldn't have to issue demands for basic humanitarian living conditions. You even turned off the coms in here. What if I get sick or needed help? I have no way to reach you."

That drew a frown from him. "I will activate the com system for you so you may only contact me. That is a fair demand."

"So is asking you to live in here with me so I'm not alone all the time."

"I don't trust you."

That made some of her anger die down a little. "I won't really kill you like I threatened. I'm not stupid. If you die, I imagine that some other cyborg will take ownership of me." She paused. "That's not on my wish list, okay? Besides, you made a deal with me over Cathy, and as long as you're alive our deal remains intact, so I know she's being taken care of by that black-haired jerk."

"Vollus is not a jerk."

"He better not be. Cathy is young and vulnerable. I'd like to talk to her soon to make sure she's really all right."

"You don't trust me?"

She stared at him. "You don't trust me either."

Iron gave a small nod of his head. "Agreed. I will let you talk to the human tomorrow. I will connect the com lines but then deactivate the link afterward. I don't want the two of you plotting an escape so your communications will be monitored."

"That's acceptable." She sighed. "Sleep with me. I'm so lonely and bored." She hesitated, hating to ask anything of him but damn, she had gone stir crazy the night before and all day. She was even happy to see her captor, it had been so bad.

"It is not a good idea."

"Why?"

He hesitated, watching her with hooded eyes. "I told you, I don't trust you."

"We just went over this! Did you turn off your ability to hear me or what? I will not attempt to kill you since I'm motivated to keep you alive and healthy. That's just simple logic, Iron. I don't want to be alone and I'm so desperate I'm asking you to stay. Don't leave me in here alone again unless you have to work. It's too quiet on this ship. I can't even hear the engines hum."

Something softened in his look. "I'll stay for a little while but then I will return to my quarters to sleep."

Irritation welled inside her. "Talk to me then."

He walked to the bed and sat. He sighed. "What do you wish to talk about?"

"What do you do for a living?"

"I command the *Star* or the *Rally,* depending on where I am needed. I'm a pilot, as I stated."

"What happened to the men you stole the *Rally* from?"

He frowned. "Why do you wish to know?"

She hesitated and then walked to his built-in dresser, opened drawers and removed one of his soft shirts to put on. The room had warmed since he'd adjusted the temperature so she was not freezing but since he was dressed she wanted to be as well. She faced him when she was covered to her mid thighs in his baggy shirt.

"I met them four years ago after they showed up at Vonder station in need of repairs. I welded the cargo blast door area to patch them up enough to make it back to Earth but they never got there."

He hesitated. "We didn't kill them if that is what you believe. We captured them and dropped them off at *Folion*."

She frowned. "Isn't that one of those hooker ships from the Monker solar system that uses...?" She stopped talking to just stare at Iron. She flushed, remembering how she'd taunted him about having a robot for a girlfriend. If he was familiar with the *Folion* then she'd hit a nerve with him. She saw his features tense and then bit her lip to not laugh. "Shit."

Iron was on his feet in a heartbeat. "I'm going to my other quarters."

Dawn moved, diving into his path. "How was I to know you liked to do girl robots?"

His jaw jerked as he clenched his teeth. "They are better than sex droids."

Confirmed! She couldn't help but grin at him. "So, how are they?"

"I'm going to my quarters." He tried to step around her.

Dawn backed up until she hit the door, bumping into it. She spread her arms out across the width. "No. Come on, you were giving me shit about sex droids but I've never used one. They are too expensive and if you could see the bunk I'm assigned to, you'd know I couldn't fit one of those things in there with me. Of course every woman on the station would be stealing

69

it and that's just gross since I don't share my sex toys." Her grin returned. "So, how is an actual artificial intelligence robot in the sack? I heard they are pretty state-of-the-art."

He crossed his arms over his chest, a telling sign that she noted he did when he was irritated. "They aren't as good as the real thing. I refuse to discuss this with you. In my defense I am not in a family unit with a female and I get assigned a lot of long missions on the *Star*."

"There aren't girl cyborgs onboard? You said you knew they were white instead of pink below the belt."

"There aren't many female cyborgs assigned on this ship but I don't like any of them. We are mostly single males aboard the *Star* and the *Rally*. Our missions are more dangerous than the other ships we have and females are rare so it's rare to risk their lives. The few who are assigned do so with special permission."

That killed some of her amusement. "What kind of things do you do? How dangerous is it to be on this ship?"

"We acquire things for our people."

"Like women?"

He hesitated. "No. You were taken for my personal use. We board vessels and salvage what we can use from them to take back to our home world, Garden. After we left Earth we found a habitable planet to settle on. We've built a city but resources there are limited except for food and water. All of our building materials and electronics have to be taken off world."

"So you're cyborg pirates?"

"We do not take people to ransom them back to Earth Government or their families and we do not sell them to the sex trade."

"You just take women to be personal sex slaves."

That drew a frown from him. "Until recently that was never the case. The lead commander, Flint, took a human first and offered me and some of the other high-ranking males the opportunity to own human women."

It took her seconds but then anger burned in Dawn as if a sudden flash fire had been ignited. "You bastard. You had no intention of cutting Cathy or me up, did you? You kidnapped my crew to make them sex slaves for your cyborg buddies, didn't you?"

He shrugged. "You wanted to believe we were ghouls and it worked in my best interest to allow you to assume you were correct. You agreed to be my sex slave. The deal is final."

"But your jerk friend who has Cathy said I was going to be taken to the doctor for a procedure. What was that about then, if not to cut me up?"

"I'm planning on taking you to see him so there is no issue of whom you belong to but work has prevented me from finding the time to make those arrangements with him."

"You're going to chip my ass? Seriously? Like parents do to children so if they get lost someone can scan them and the readers say who they belong to?"

He regarded her silently. He didn't deny that was exactly what he was going to do and it really irritated her. Pet owners, along with parents, did the same thing with their animals. She guessed it must have really amused him to know she was terrified of being flayed like a fish when instead he just wanted to have an implanted data chip shot into her ass.

"You tricked me."

He let his hands fall to his sides. "The result would have been the same. I chose you from the *Piera*."

Shock tore through her. "You chose me?"

He nodded. "We didn't take all fourteen women. We could have but we just took the women we chose. Vollus chose your young friend and I chose you."

"Why me?" She was still shocked.

He hesitated. "You were smaller than I would have liked but your hair drew me."

Dawn reached up to absently finger a lock of her red hair. "Seriously? Why?"

"You are as rare as I am." He paused. "Not many humans or cyborgs have our coloring. I thought that if I ever bred you that our children would end up with that coloring."

Her mouth was hanging open and the second she realized it, she jerked her jaw up to press her lips together. Her mind was going a mile a minute, trying to take it all in. One word hit her like a brick. "Breed? As in have kids?" She pressed back against the door.

That frown again marred his lips again. "What other definition of breeding do you know, to even ask that question? Of course I am discussing reproduction."

"I'm thirty-six!"

He shrugged. "Your point being?"

"I don't want kids. My five sisters all had a bunch of them when they were young and I didn't for a reason. I have seventeen nieces and nephews so if I want to play mommy I just babysit some of them for my siblings when I'm on Earth and I'm cured instantly of feeling my biological clock ticking. No way will I agree to have kids." Her gaze flew up and down his big body. "And I sure as hell wouldn't have them with you."

All expression left his face. He was motionless but then she noticed his hands fisted at his side. "You don't think I'm a fit breeding partner because I'm a cyborg?" He growled deep in the back of his throat. "You just stripped me and asked me to touch you yet you think I am not worthy of implanting your eggs?"

"Implanting my eggs?" She gapped at him. "This has nothing to do with you being gray, damn it. Look in a mirror. You're the size of a hover cycle and if we're talking giving birth, think about it. What were you at birth? Twenty pounds?"

He frowned. "I wasn't birthed. I was grown in a lab."

Dawn's heart pounded. "So you plan on taking my eggs and having children grown like you were in some lab after you knock up my eggs? I refuse! If I have kids, not that I will, but if I *did* I'd have them the old-fashioned way."

Iron moved, crowding her space as he went chest to face with her. She stared up at him as he put his hands flat on the door on both sides of her,

73

pinning her where she stood. He looked furious as he glared down into her eyes.

"I didn't ask you what you wanted. If I decide to breed with you then we will breed the old-fashioned way, as you put it. I'll activate my sperm and have Doc examine you to fix any problems he finds with you that may hinder my implanting your eggs."

She had to swallow hard as a lump formed in her throat. "I didn't agree to that. I said I'd be your slave, not a baby maker."

Iron's face lowered until they were almost nose-to-nose. "You're property, Dawn. The sooner you realize that your life is no longer your own, the sooner you can learn your place."

Fear and anger flooded her. She went with anger and instantly tried to shove him back. She caught him unaware, actually made him stumble a few feet, and she kicked out at him. Her bare foot hit his hip, knocking him back more. Dawn glared at him.

"I always have a say, Iron. You learn *that*."

He rubbed his hip, returning her glare. "Do you want me to put you over my knee and spank you to teach you that I am in control?"

"Try it, asshole. I haven't been spanked since I was ten years old and hid my dad's favorite fusion wrench for two weeks to get even with him."

Iron lunged forward. Dawn ducked but she knew he had missed her within inches. She ran and leapt on his bed, turning so her back hit the corner. She glared at the big bastard where he hesitated at the corner of the bed. He looked irritated.

"I can reach you easily there."

"Try it, Iron. I dare you."

He grabbed for her. Dawn pushed off and propelled her body at him to jump on him. She hit his chest and screamed as he grunted. He stumbled back, obviously not expecting her to attack him. It happened fast but Dawn knew it was going to hurt the second she realized he'd been off balance and her momentum hit him too hard. He went backward, falling and she went with him.

He jerked her before they hit the floor, yanking her lower on his body so he took the brunt of the impact with Dawn landing on top of him. She heard a cracking sound and scrambled to get off him before he could grab hold of her. His big body had cushioned her fall so she wasn't hurt in the least as she rolled off him and got to her feet, spinning to face him as she backed up quickly.

Iron lay on the floor not moving, his eyes closed. Dawn backed up almost into the foam cleansing room to put as much space between the two of them as possible. Her gaze fixed on the still cyborg, waiting for him to open his eyes and come after her. He stayed down as the seconds passed, his eyes remained closed, and the only movement was the rise and fall of his chest.

"Damn it, Iron. I'm not stupid. You're playing possum."

She stood there, knowing it was a trick. He'd already proved he wasn't above screwing with her head to get his way. She bit her lip as seconds passed into a good minute. He was patient, she'd give him that. She didn't take her attention from him but then something on the floor caught her eye. The red substance that discolored the floor had her alarmed in a heartbeat.

"Iron?" She moved then, almost diving for him to collapse on her knees next to him. It was definitely blood she saw next to his ear on the hard floor. Her hands shook as she reached for him. "Computer? Emergency Response. I need a medic!" She gripped his face and waited for the computer to respond but it didn't.

Frustration welled in her as she stared down at Iron's face. His skin tone looked a little more on the white side at that moment. Her fingers gently eased into his soft hair and tried to find the wound but with his hair braided it was difficult to do. She wanted to scream for help but she knew how thick the walls were and it would mute out all sounds, which meant no one would hear her.

"Damn it, Iron. Open those beautiful eyes for me, baby. I didn't mean to hurt you. Of all the lame-ass things to do, you disabled the computer completely, didn't you? I can't get you help."

She finally found the wound. It was small, just a gash at the back of his head. She carefully tried to roll him but she couldn't since he was too heavy to budge. All she could do was carefully turn his head, hoping she wasn't hurting him more and her fingers were shaking the entire time as she unbraided his hair. He had long, curly, bright red hair and she would have enjoyed seeing all of it as she freed the last of it but she was too worried about the downed man. She didn't want him to die.

Very gently, she separated his hair where his scalp was cut to discover it really was small but head wounds bled a lot. She pressed her fingertip to it and held pressure there. Her gaze fixed on his profile with his face turned her way.

"I'm sorry, Iron. I didn't think I could really hurt you. You're like a house with legs. If you just open your eyes, I promise I won't tackle you anymore. I might even let you tap my ass with one of your abnormally large hands once or twice. Just wake up for me, open those beautiful blues and glare at me."

She nearly jumped when he opened his eyes as if he'd heard her. She stared into them and relief flooded her. She smiled. "Don't move. I'm so sorry. You're bleeding. It's not bad but you scared me."

He lay still as he watched her silently and allowed her to keep her finger pressed against his damaged scalp. He didn't talk so Dawn did.

"I really didn't think I could hurt you. Are you okay?" She held up three fingers in front of his face with her free hand. "How many do you see?"

Alarm was instant on Dawn's part when he didn't answer. "Did you scramble something? Look, repeat what I say, okay? Emergency Response, we need a medic. Can you say that for me, baby? Please say it. The damn computer won't activate for me and you need help."

He blinked at her but still said nothing. Alarm turned to fear as she gazed into his eyes, completely worried. "Iron, you have to tell the computer to get help. You disabled the computer from responding to me. Can you activate your transmitter in your head and link to the computer to get help? Try, okay? You hit your head on the floor and you were knocked unconscious. You need a medic. If you can't—"

77

She tore her gaze from his, darting her eyes around the room and spotting the fire sensor in the corner of the ceiling. She bit her lip as her mind frantically worked trying to find a solution. It hit her then and she came up with a plan.

"I could start a fire. That would alert the computer to send responders." She looked down at him. "That's what I'll do, okay? I'm going to have to fuck up the door pad to get access to some live wires but I can make some sparks to make fire. I'll torch one of your shirts. It won't spread or anything but it will put off enough smoke to trigger the alarm." She eased her finger from his wound, focused on it and was relieved when it didn't start actively bleeding again. She nodded at him. "Just hang on, baby. I'm going to get you the help you need."

She moved to get to her feet but Iron's hand suddenly shot out and grabbed her, his hand wrapping around the back of her neck. She gasped as he pulled her down close to his face, struggling to not tip forward and fall on him as her hands shot out to brace on the floor next to him. He stopped pulling when they were nearly nose-to-nose.

"Don't start a fire."

"Tell the computer to get you a medic."

He licked his lips as he stared into her eyes, studying them. "You care that I am hurt and you want to bring help to me."

"Of course I do. Tell the damn computer to get you a medic. Your head is bleeding."

He closed his eyes for a second and then opened them again. "I'm fine, Dawn. I ran a scan. I have that ability. I'm functioning normally."

"You whacked your head hard and it knocked you out so you're not fine."

He took a deep breath and then his other hand moved, wrapping around her waist. He pulled her on top of his chest. It stunned her as she stared into his eyes a second before he rolled them both, her back ending up against the floor with a big cyborg pinning her flat. He shifted his body, easing down her as he fit his thighs between hers. His long, flowing, bright red hair fell forward over one of his shoulders, pooling on the floor next to her face. She glanced at the beauty of all that glorious, fiery red hair and then she gazed into his eyes. He had her caged under him but his elbows took his weight so he wasn't crushing her.

"Iron? What are you doing? Order the computer to summon help."

He just stared into her eyes for long seconds before his mouth lowered. Dawn realized his intent a second before his full lips lightly brushed her shocked, parted ones. She closed her eyes instantly and her hands gripped the leather of his shirt at the curve of his shoulders as firm lips pushed hers wider apart before his warm tongue breached her mouth.

He explored her slowly at first, their tongues gliding against each other but then his kiss grew bold, more dominant, to take charge of the kiss. It was easy for Dawn to get lost in him. Iron might act a bit cold and unfeeling but the way his tongue and mouth possessed her showed her another side of him as the passion flared between them. The sweet melting together of their lips turned into something more frantic as her body ignited with need. She shifted her hands and delved her fingers into his loose hair, holding him closer as she turned her head a little more to align their mouths more firmly.

Iron pulled back, breaking the kiss. Dawn forced her eyes open to stare up into his gorgeous gaze, unable to miss the same desire she was experiencing mirrored there.

Iron lifted up, bracing his weight on one hand so he could reach between them. She heard his zipper and lifted her legs, wrapping them around his hips as he freed his cock from his pants. She was wet and ready as he shoved the shirt she wore up to her stomach to get it out of the way. They never looked away from each other as he came down on her slowly, his thighs spreading a little more to adjust his hips to the right angle so when he lowered, his hard cock pressed dead on against her pussy. He entered her with one slow motion.

Pleasure was instant and Dawn wiggled her hips while her legs locked tighter around his wide hips to pull him even closer and deeper inside her body. *He is heaven and hell*, she thought as she moaned his name.

The floor was hard but she didn't care if she ended up with bruises as Iron started to move on her, fucking her in slow but deep thrusts with his powerful hips. Dawn released his hair so she didn't pull it and instead clawed the leather of his shirt to cling to him. She just allowed the passion to flow through her. She started into his gorgeous eyes. Emotions played there openly for her to watch. Iron was not trying to hide how much she affected him or he didn't realize his guard was down as he moved on her.

"Iron," she clawed at his shirt frantically, gripping him. "Don't stop."

A soft growl came from his throat as he suddenly stopped moving on her. Dawn wanted to scream. Had he stopped just because she'd told him not to? He shoved up on a hand.

"Release my hips."

"No."

"I want you on top. I'd roll us but your legs are around my hips. Release me and climb on me."

She unwrapped her legs and regretted when he withdrew from her body. He rolled to his back, shoved his pants down his legs more and then turned his head to watch Dawn sit up and get to her knees.

Iron was damn impressive when he was hard and on his back. The man was hung. She straddled his hips, realizing her knees were barely going to reach the hard floor as she crouched over him. He gripped her hips as he easily lifted her into position over his throbbing cock. She gasped but then loudly moaned as he maneuvered her right onto him, making her take his cock back into her body until he was completely sheathed inside her pussy.

"Oh God," she whispered.

"Am I hurting you?"

She stared down into his eyes. "No. You feel so good."

He lifted his knees, bending them, and braced his feet on the floor. "Lean back against my thighs to support your back."

She leaned back as he ordered before he started to move. His hips thrust up, lifting her body with his as his hands on her hips lifted and slammed her down on him then working his hips so he nearly withdrew from her body before he slammed home again.

All Dawn could do was grab hold of his forearms, lean farther back against his thighs and cry out as he fucked her. It was amazing, and as he increased the pace, the blissful goodness of being taken by him turned into sheer ecstasy. Her vaginal walls started to clench and the climax built. Iron was so hard, so strong, and he kept going. He drew her deeper into the web of passion with him until she threw her head back, forcing her to look away from his handsome face. She screamed out as the climax tore through her. Under her, Iron's hands drew her down where he held her as only his hips worked now, his cock's strokes short and jerky. She could feel when he came, felt him filling her with his release, and she dropped her head down to watch him.

Iron in the thrall of passion was a sight she never wanted to forget as pure emotion twisted his features. His lips parted as he groaned loudly, his head tipped back. His big body slowly relaxed under her, his mouth closing, and she watched his eyes open to gaze into hers. For those precious moments, she saw genuine warmth staring back at her.

Dawn leaned down, flattened her body on his torso and looked away from him to press her cheek to his chest. His heart pounded under her ear as she lay there on him, both of them catching their breath. She smiled when his arms wrapped around her to hold her. She could stay that way for a long time. She was warm, sated, and happy.

"Are you sure your head is okay?"

His hands rubbed her back. "If it will make you feel better I'll have Doc look me over first thing when his next shift starts."

She nodded against his skin. "I'll worry less if you do. Thank you."

He didn't move for a long time, just allowed her lie on him with their bodies still joined. When he finally did move, she experienced regret as she sat up to get off him. She hated separating their bodies as he helped her to her feet. He stood up next to her. Dawn lifted her chin and held out her hand.

"Please stay with me."

He frowned but took her hand in his. "Lie down. I'll hold you for a little while."

She climbed into his bed and he got in with her, the bed small so they had to curl tightly together on their sides. He spooned her in front of him, one arm under her head to pillow her cheek, his other arm wrapped around her.

"I like this," Dawn admitted, pressing more firmly against his naked body.

Iron hesitated. "It is pleasant."

She yawned. "Stay with me, Iron. Sleep with me."

He just held her and refused to answer. She hoped he'd change his mind about spending all night with her. She yawned again, tired from the stress she'd been under and from pacing his room.

Chapter Six

Dawn clenched her teeth as she glared at Iron. "Something has to change."

Iron tilted his head while he stared at her with narrowed eyes. "I see nothing wrong with our arrangement."

"You wouldn't." She shook her head. "You leave me all day and then you just spend a few hours with me. I don't see you again until you bring me breakfast and then you leave for your shift. I'm going batty."

"I brought you entertainment. You can watch holographic films and you seem to enjoy music since you are always listening to it when I come in."

"I'm going crazy in this room. At least take me for a walk. You don't even have a window in your quarters. Staring at black space is better than these damn walls, Iron. Do you want me to beg? Is that it? I've lost track of days. How long have I been here? How long ago was it when you let me talk to Cathy for those two minutes so I knew she was fine?"

He frowned. "It isn't important, Dawn."

Hot tears burned behind her eyes. The sex between them was terrific. He was a talented lover and he was always willing to please her. She had no complaints there but he wouldn't sleep in the bed with her and he refused to use the foam cleansing unit in the room so she could see his hair free again. He kept her at a distance unless they were hot and heavy during sex. He held her afterward for a while but the second she fell asleep, she knew he left her. It was progress that he cuddled after sex but she wanted more.

She walked over to where he sat on the bed. She hesitated and then just straddled his lap. She saw shock widen his eyes as she gripped his shoulders and adjusted her legs to wrap them around his hips so she was comfortable. His hands gripped her butt as he stared into her eyes.

"You want sex now? You haven't finished your dinner yet and you need to eat."

"Do you want me to beg?" Her voice broke and she hated it. "I will at this point. Please, Iron? Take me for a walk. I need out of this room." She saw his frown deepen and her heart sank, knowing he was going to refuse.

He shook his head. "It is not a good idea."

"If you don't then I won't eat any more." She hesitated. "I mean it. If I have to make myself sick to get taken to medical, I'll do it at this point. Do I have to break my arm or something to get out of here even for something like that? I'm to that point, damn it."

He searched her expression. "You're serious."

"Duh. I've been saying it for days and I mean it. I'm going crazy, Iron. I'm a mechanic. I'm used to doing things, fixing things, and now I sit here all day just waiting for you." She curled into his chest, tucking her face in the crook of his neck, inhaling his wonderful masculine scent, which she had grown to love. "Please? Just a walk up and down the hallway out there would be better than this."

His hands rose to the small of her back. "All right, Dawn. I'll take you out of here for a few hours."

Excitement and surprise had her lifting her head to grin at him. "Really? Thank you!" She gripped his face and planted a kiss on his stunned lips. She moved and climbed off him. "I'll put on my boots and my pants!" She almost hopped across the room. "I'm so excited!"

"There are a few conditions you must agree to first."

His words killed her joy as she turned to face him. Their gazes locked. "What conditions?"

"I want you branded."

"Branded?"

He opened his shirt to reveal the tattoos on his upper chest. They were small. "These are my marks, my name in the cyborg language we created. If I take you out there for a few hours you need to carry my mark on your body to show to the other males that you are mine."

"I wondered what those were but I haven't asked." She stared at the black tattoos and then her gaze slid to lock with his. "Why? I don't like tattoos. They are fine for you," she said quickly. "I just don't want them on my body."

He stood up. "Then I can't take you out of the room."

She glared at him. "Seriously? Tattoos are expensive to remove. What happens when—" She slammed her lips together before she finished that sentence. One day she'd escape and then she'd have to pay some doctor to remove them to wipe away the memory of her time with Iron. "I just don't want them."

"When what?" He slowly stood up.

"How about when you get tired of me and want a new slave? Then I'd still have your name on me and hell, I won't put any man's name on my body."

"I will not grow tired of you. I will never give you away or release you." He took a step closer. "I own you. You will carry my name on your body."

Lifting her chin, Dawn stared at him. Her heart fluttered a little over his declaration of never releasing her. They stared at each other for a long time before Iron crossed his arms over his chest, the habit she knew meant he was frustrated.

"We could argue and yell." He paused. "Or I could knock you out and have it done while you are drugged. It is going to happen."

"Really?" She crossed her arms over her chest, shifted her feet until she mimicked his stance completely. "Is that so?"

"That is a fact. You can either agree or I will make you."

"You know what? Every time I decide you're not a total asshole you pull this shit."

"I won't take your defiance."

"And I won't let you put your name on me."

They glared at each other until Iron finally spoke. "I am going to go work out. While I'm gone you can consider your options. If you want to be able to leave this room you will do what I want."

Frustration, anger, and desperation all hit her at once. She moved and blocked his way to the door. "Don't you dare just stalk out. Don't give me hope that I'm going to get the hell out of this room, dangle it in front of me, and then take it away."

"You heard your options. You may agree to take my brand or move out of the way, Dawn."

She blinked back tears. She'd be damned if she let him see that he'd made her cry. Iron frowned when she didn't budge. His arms dropped to his sides and he took a few steps toward her, stopping inches in front of her.

"Move, Dawn. I am going to give you some time to weigh your options. When I return in the morning we'll discuss this again."

"In the morning? You're not coming back tonight?"

He shook his head. "I think you need the time to reflect on your situation."

"You're punishing me in other words," she hotly accused. "Damn it, Iron. Don't do this to me."

"You are doing it to yourself. If you would just agree we would both be walking out of this room right now."

"I have pride," she said softly. "Don't do this. Don't force this on me. I'll hate you."

A muscle in his jaw flexed and his features softened. "I don't wish that."

"Then let's find a compromise we can both live with."

"What kind of compromise?"

She drew a blank for a few seconds and then swallowed. She'd never thought she'd ever get a tattoo in her life. *Then again*, she thought, *I never thought I'd find myself in this kind of situation.* A sudden idea entered her mind.

"I'll get a tattoo if you get one as well."

Dark red eyebrows arched. "I already have them."

"You want me to have your name on my body then I want my name put on your body. That's fair."

Iron couldn't hide his shock at her suggestion. He stepped back, a frown marring his features. "Is this a joke?"

"Is it? You tell me. I'll agree to take your name on my skin if you take mine."

His eyes closed and he took a deep breath before they opened again. "Just Dawn or do I have to carry your last name as well?"

It was her turn to be shocked. She hadn't honestly thought he'd even consider it. "What do your tattoos mean?" She glanced at them. "I sure can't read them."

"My name." He touched his right side. "This is Iron and this..." He touched the marks on the left. "This is my rank."

"Rank?"

"I'm an original, the first of my kind. We're marked for generations and it shows my importance in my society as a commander of a ship."

Licking her lips, Dawn swallowed hard. "Just my first name would work. Do I have to have your rank put on me too?"

"Yes."

She looked at the tattoos on him again. They weren't ugly or anything, just different, similar to ancient tribal markings. Her attention went back to his face to find that he still watched her. She put out her hand to him.

"It's a deal then. I'll take your name on me and you'll put my name on you."

Iron glanced down at her hand and then took it. She expected him to shake on it but instead he lifted her hand and to her surprise, he turned it palm up to brush a soft kiss on her wrist. He released her, jerked his head at the door, and sighed.

"We'll go see Doc right now."

Excitement hit Dawn at the prospect of leaving Iron's quarters. She really had lost track of days. She was sure at least a week had passed. The doors slid open behind her, thanks to Iron silently signaling with his mind. She wished she had that ability, one she would find useful in her line of work, and turned to almost run out of the room. Just stepping through the doors into the hallway was exhilarating.

A hand clamped down on her upper arm, Iron's fingers curling around it, and she stared up at him as he stepped up beside her. She gave him a dirty look.

"I'm not going to run."

"I didn't say you would. If you were considering it, there is nowhere to go. All the emergency pods have been deactivated."

She kept silent as they walked, not about to explain to him that she could easily steal one of his precious life pods from the *Star*. She could hotwire anything with an engine. Of course she was also smart. While the

Star's life pods were fast, they weren't built with large fuel tanks. She would burn up too much fuel trying to outrun the *Star* and when her reserves were low, she'd have to slow. The other ship would then be able to catch up with her easily and capture her again.

She wasn't a novice in space either. She had no idea where she was but she figured she was in deep space, far from the regular outposts and space stations. Cyborgs would want to stay far off Earth Government radar. The only things out in deep space were obviously cyborgs and a hell of a lot of mutated pirates. She shivered as she walked, never wanting to come across them again.

Iron stopped walking and stared down at her. "Are you well?"

"I'm fine."

"You looked frightened. I won't allow anyone to harm you, Dawn. Do you doubt my ability to protect you?"

"You said something about the life pod and I was thinking how stupid it would be to take one, if you want the truth. I'm guessing we're pretty far off the beaten path of travel routes so there have to be a lot of pirates out this way."

"Yes. There are. They like to stay far from the travel routes because they know the standard is to shoot at them upon sensor detection. You need not worry about the *Star* being attacked. The *Rally* and the *Star* are a team, both ship and shuttle travel together. It dissuades even the more aggressive pirates to not attempt an attack."

She nodded. "You're smart. Unfortunately, those crazy bastards rarely do the sane thing. They've attacked the Vonder a few times over the past year."

A frown marred Iron's lips as he hit the button to call for the lift. "The Vonder is a large station. It would be suicide for them to attack it. We wouldn't even do that."

"Yeah, well, nobody said pirates were bright. We have a kick-ass defense system but its slow getting parts out to us from Earth sometimes. We had four of our lasers go down after we took some fragment hits from a passing comet so we had a blindside that one of their ships slid through before we could turn the station so we were in spin mode to continuously fire at them."

Iron watched her with that same frown on his face as the lift doors opened and he led her inside. "Did they breach the Vonder?"

"Uh, no, not in the way you'd think." Dawn sighed. "I was outside in a space suit repairing hull dents we'd sustained from those same fragment hits we took when they attacked. I barely made it into the docking doors before they were hooking up and blowing out the hatch I'd just come through, to gain entry. You know what I did to the *Rally's* docking room? Think bigger. I blew out a section of hull after they boarded that area of the station to keep them from reaching the living areas with my crew."

Iron looked stunned as he stared mutely at her.

"I watched them die, heard them screaming until the air was gone. It was hell. I had to vent their remains before I started to patch the hole so I could seal it up and reestablish oxygen. I had less than twenty minutes of air in my tanks by the time I was done. If the patch hadn't held I would have suffocated too. I couldn't walk outside to the docking port on the other side of the station since we were spinning to keep those bastards off us. My tether wouldn't have been strong enough. My ass would have been tossed out into space."

His expression turned grim. "Your job was very dangerous, Dawn. I am glad you will never do it again."

She wasn't about to tell him that once she escaped from him that going back to the Vonder was exactly what she'd do. It was her home now and they needed her. Other mechanics had come and gone in the past eight years to assist her but they never stayed. It was a lonely, shitty job with too many hours and too many repairs to keep up with but the pay was too good to walk away from.

The lift doors slid open when it stopped. Dawn peered out into the large cargo area and to her stunned disbelief saw over a dozen cyborg males in skimpy, thin outfits tossing each other around on thick mats on the floor. Iron gripped her arm again to tug her out of the lift.

"We exercise here to keep physically maintained. Do not be alarmed. The fighting is not genuine."

The men stopped what they were doing as Dawn was pulled into the room. All attention focused on her and she glanced at each male, seeing their open interest instantly. Iron muttered something so softly she missed his words.

"What?"

"I was hoping that none of them would be working out at this hour."

"You're going to give me a tattoo in here? Seriously?"

Iron jerked his head. "Look."

She followed his gaze and saw that in the far corner a Med area had been set up. She was in for a shock when a human older man walked into the room. His white hair put him at over fifty in age, a thin framed man in good physical shape from the firmness of his muscular arms. A scar was evident, which had her guessing someone had sliced open his face with a thick blade once. The guy openly stared at Dawn for a few seconds before he shot a dirty look at Iron.

"Another one? Seriously? I'm going to run out of magnetic ink, damn it. I told Flint I'm low on it after I branded the last woman brought to me."

"Is there enough?" Iron tensed. "It's important to me."

The doctor hesitated. "Yeah." The man turned his attention on Dawn, studying her.

She stared back at him. "You are owned by them too?"

The man shook his head before he turned away, going to a cupboard along the wall. "No. I was rescued and freed by them. I was assigned to the *Star* when she left Earth's orbit after she was cleared for flight. I was one of three medical staff members assigned to her." He rummaged and pulled out a few things. "The *Star* was taken by pirates and they killed most of the crew, ransomed some of the lucky ones back to Earth, or sold them to some of the outer posts as sex workers." He set four cases on one of the only two med beds. "I'm the only one they kept aboard since I'm a medic. They kept me pretty damn busy with how messed up they are physically."

Surprise tore through Dawn. "Pirates were able to take this thing? How did they do that?" Dawn frowned at Iron. "You said this was a Class-A ship. That means it's fully armored, has state-of-the-art defensive weapons and it's not that old. As far as ships go it's a baby so it's got to be pretty impressive technology. How were pirates able to get control of it?"

The medic cleared his throat. "Our captain was straight out of the academy. His father was some big shot who got his precious boy assigned." He glanced at Dawn. "Call me Doc. You both need to remove your shirts." He opened another case. "As I was saying, the captain was green and an idiot. We ran into a group of pirates with four ships docked together in a cluster who instantly surrendered as we approached them claiming they were dead in space with mechanical failures. Captain Tillis wouldn't listen when the crew tried to tell him to just kill them. Instead he docked the *Star* directly to them, thinking he was saving lives, and of course they attacked the second they were aboard. They'd had more of their ships hiding behind a moon, had filled those four linked ships over capacity from all the men from the hidden ships so at least fifty of those bastards were able to walk right onto the *Star*."

"Shit." Dawn shook her head. "Didn't your captain scan for life signs first or have security teams ready to open fire on them if it was a trick?"

"Obviously not. I said you both need to remove your shirts."

Dawn turned her head to look at Iron, seeing that he'd removed his shirt. He frowned at her, waiting for her to comply but instead Dawn turned to glance at the other cyborgs across the large room, silently staring directly at her. She swallowed.

"Um, isn't there somewhere private we can do this?" She looked back at Iron, her voice lowering. "They are watching me."

"It's a public area." Iron shrugged his broad shoulders. "I can't make them leave and this is where Med is set up. The original Med was destroyed in the battle that took place when the *Star* was taken over by pirates. We restored it but Doc says he likes working here better because he always has company with the men using this area for training."

"And I'm right on hand if they get a little rough with each other." Doc chuckled. "No way in hell do I want to be stuck spending my days staring at nothing but walls."

Dread filled Dawn as she carefully removed her shirt while she made sure that her breasts remained covered. If she was on the Vonder she would have shucked all of her clothes in a heartbeat but those weren't other women staring at her. She glanced back at Iron to see that he was silently watching her still.

"You've got my back, right? You said all your men are single. Me stripping isn't going to cause any shit? None of them are going to want to move closer to try to touch me, are they?"

"I made it clear that you are mine." Iron's voice went deeper. "Do you think I can't defend you if there is a problem?"

She sized up his large body. "Nope. You look pretty able to kick some ass." She clutched the material against her breasts and faced the doctor. "What now, Doc?"

"Have a seat. I am going to use an imager to scan and copy Iron's markings and then I'm going to hook it to this neat device that will form to

96

the area we want tattooed. It will hook into the imager, inject tiny needles into your skin and remove tiny bits of fat tissue to replace it with magnetic ink." He paused. "The wrap can manipulate the ink under your skin once it's injected and force it to move where it's needed to copy the image it wants imprinted. You'll smell a little burning flesh scent but that will be the tiny bit of fat tissue it removes being disposed of." He paused again. "Am I clear? You have to hold still. If you have a problem with doing that, say so now and I'll give you something to help."

Dawn stared at the doctor. "I've heard of magnetic ink tats. I get the concept. I just wasn't sure how it was done. Is it going to be painful? That's all I care to know."

"You'll feel the needles and I've been told you can feel some weird sensations while the ink is being pulled to the right skin locations but nobody has ever complained about real pain."

She climbed up on the med bed and kept the shirt clutched to her breasts to keep them covered. She looked at Iron. "Don't forget to tell him to put my name on your body. That was the deal."

"Her name?" Doc gasped, his head turning back and forth, staring at each of them.

Iron sighed loudly, an annoyed expression on his features. "I made an agreement with Dawn. If she would agree to my brand on her body without a fight, I agreed to have her brand put on my body. She deemed that fair and I saw the logic in her demand."

Doc's eyebrows arched. "Wow. Okay." He turned his shocked expression to Dawn. "What do you want on him and where?"

97

Looking at Iron's chest and arms, she tried to think of where she wanted her name. Her gaze went lower and then lifted to his face. Iron stared silently at her. She glanced into his gorgeous blue eyes and knew in that second where she wanted her name on his body. As tempting as it was to ask the medic to put it on Iron's beefy ass just for the teasing ability to tell him she owned his ass too, she instead chose another location.

"I'd like Dawn put in small letters on his lower stomach right next to his hipbone. That way it's hidden unless he's naked." She touched the area on her lower stomach, indicating where she wanted Iron marked. "Right there."

Doc looked stunned, his eyes were wide open and his mouth hanging open a bit. He jerked his gaze from Dawn to stare openly in disbelief at Iron.

Dawn watched Iron closely, wondering if he'd protest her wanting the tattoo there. He met her gaze but then looked at Doc and nodded as he agreed to allow her name to go on his body where she wanted it. She hated to admit it but Dawn was a little touched that he didn't argue the point. When she left him and he moved on to another slave, that woman would have to look at her name on his body every time he stripped naked. She'd always be a reminder to him that he'd once made love to her. It was fitting since she'd never be able to take off her shirt without being reminded that she'd once been owned by Iron Cyborg.

The medic nodded. "Okay. Let's get this show on the road, folks."

Fear hit Dawn as she watched Doc point a small camera at Iron who turned his body and bowed down a little so every angle of his tattoos were recorded. She wasn't into pain and never had been. She was tempted to ask Doc to give her something for it in case it did hurt but then she looked at Iron's chest. She bet he hadn't asked for painkillers when he'd had those put there.

It was a matter of principle, she decided. She was tough, she could take it and she would. When Doc moved toward her to put the big, heavy wrap around her shoulders, she didn't protest but she did tense. He was careful to cover her from neck to lower ribs before he asked for her shirt.

"Why?"

"You're covered and it will scan your ribs to help map bone placement to exactly mark you the way Iron is."

She eased the shirt from beneath the wrap and released it from the death grip she'd had on it. It reminded her of when she was a small child and had a favorite blanket she'd slept with. Wherever Dawn had gone, her blankie had been with her until she was about five years old. She turned her head and locked gazes with Iron. *God, I hope this doesn't hurt*, she silently prayed, not looking away from Iron's watchful gaze.

The wrap tightened even more, hugging her in a stronger embrace. She kept her breathing to a minimum, only taking shallow breaths.

"Hold still," Doc warned. "You don't want to mess this up."

"I won't move," she promised softly.

Doc hooked the camera into a port on the wrap with a small cord. He hit a button, his gaze lifting. "Here we go. Just hold real steady."

The needles went into her skin. Small pricks of pain but it was tolerable. The wrap vibrated slightly and something cold injected into her and she realized it had to be the magnetic ink. *So far, so good*, she thought.

99

In seconds an uncomfortable sensation tingled as if something wiggled under her skin. It didn't hurt or tickle but it was noticeable. The wrap vibrated more, the smell of something burning filled the air but she didn't panic, expecting it since Doc had told her that it wasn't her skin frying.

In minutes it was over. The wrap had to be gently pried from her skin. Iron moved forward instantly to pick up her shirt. He held it up to hide her breasts as she was freed from the device. She looked down, staring at identical tattoos to Iron's in black ink over the curve of her shoulders. The skin was slightly red.

Doc sighed. "Now it's your turn, Iron. Lower your pants."

Chapter Seven

Dawn ate her food, watching Iron closely. He had come into the room in a foul mood. She swallowed her bite of steak and sipped her juice. "What is going on? Rough day at work?"

Iron hesitated before he answered. "It is this latest mission that we are on. There is so much to do and it's proven more difficult than I first estimated."

He never talked about work. She had tried to pull details from him but he always brushed off her questions. She decided to try again. She'd discuss paint colors with the guy if he'd just talk to her. Usually he'd bring her food, they'd spend a few hours getting close and personal, something she looked forward to, and the second she nodded off to sleep afterward he'd leave the room to return to his quarters down the hall. She knew that because she had faked sleep once—that had taken practice since he could read her so well—just to see how long he'd stay. He'd left immediately.

"What is the mission?"

To her shock, he answered her. "We are rescuing cyborgs off a planet surface. Their ship was thought lost to us when we originally fled Earth. We had to separate and they never arrived to rejoin us."

"I'm not real familiar with all that happened. I dropped out of school and history wasn't my thing. I know that you were created for some deep space missions nobody else wanted to take." She pushed the tray aside, done with her meal. "They wanted pilots to go out looking for new planets farther than we had previously explored."

Iron sat on the bed a few feet from her. "When they created us they thought we would be living robots. They determined we wouldn't have souls but they were wrong. We have emotions and think for ourselves." He paused. "They implanted chips in our heads, trying to stop those functions but we were able to work around them to reestablish the parts of our brains they tried to block us from. We just hid it better. Once we realized they were sending us on death missions, to spend our lives aboard shuttles designed to never return to Earth but instead to send data back to them, we rebelled by demanding human status. We wanted rights that other humans had. We tried to do it by following their laws. We found council that spoke on our behalf but we were deemed property, not fit to have rights or the ability to say no to their orders."

Sympathy welled inside Dawn as she reached out to touch him. "They were wrong to do that. You're living beings and hell, other than the color of your skin, you are human."

The tense expression on his features softened. He moved his hand, placing it over hers to curl around it. "We are in agreement there. We might have genetic enhancements and have technology added to our bodies but we are human on every basic level."

"So Earth Government turned down your requests because you were free labor they didn't want to give up."

A firm nod of his head indicated he agreed with Dawn's blunt statement. "They mandated we follow orders or we would be terminated.

We went on strike, refusing to take our shifts or attend our classes. They arrested us and took us to detention centers. What they didn't factor in was that they'd given some of us the ability to send and receive data so we might have been confined to holding cells in small numbers but they took us to the same holding facility."

"You could silently communicate with each other."

"Yes." He paused. "They deemed their cyborg project a huge failure and realized we posed a threat since we were not only great pilots but they'd made our bodies much stronger and durable for long-term space travel, making us physically superior if we chose to declare war on them. From what some of us overheard from guards and the data streams we were able to pick up, we were able to figure out that they were going to mass execute all cyborgs within weeks."

"Oh my God," Dawn whispered. "All of you? Not just the ones they thought would be trouble to them?"

"All of us. They were trying to decide if they should gas us in our cells or poison our food. There was a hot debate going on about it from the coms we were able to pick up that were transmitted."

"Son of a bitch." Dawn inched closer to him. "So you escaped."

"We did. They'd given us access to a lot of the shuttles for training purposes but they failed to revoke our access after they locked us up. It was an oversight on their part that helped us. We revolted in unison since we were able to link to enough of our kind that they could coordinate with others in their holding cells. We'd been docile before that day so they weren't prepared for our attack."

"You stole their shuttles."

He nodded. "We filled them and lifted off the planet. Some of us had trained on the *Moonslip*, the *Georgeton*, and the *Barclay* so we had interaction with some of their crews. We contacted them, pretending that we'd been cleared for duty and they allowed us to dock without raising alarms. From there we took over the ships, put the humans in emergency pods to return to Earth since we didn't want to kill unless we had to. By then Earth Government realized what had happened and were scrambling defensive fighters from the surface to attack the starships."

"Shit."

"We had to leave some of our kind behind but they'd been freed from the detention center. We fled the solar system and split up so we would be harder to track and attack with force. We put most of our women on the *Moonslip*. It was a faster ship with the best defensive capability. Our women weren't as strong as we were in battle so our priority was protecting them and giving them the best chance at survival."

Dawn was touched. Cyborgs were better than humans in her mind. Most human men would have slit someone's throat to get the best ship in that instance. Chivalry had died a long time ago on Earth but obviously not inside the cyborg males who had made certain their women had the better chance of not being blown out of space.

"We were supposed to meet up in the Raxtor system in five months." Iron took a deep breath. "The *Moonslip* never showed. We thought they were lost or destroyed. It was a severe blow to my people. Eighty-two percent of our women who had fled Earth were on that ship."

"Shit." Dawn was horrified for him.

"We located Garden, settled on the planet, and started to rebuild our lives." He paused. "Our males greatly outnumber our females so we've had to adjust to those circumstances. It's been difficult for all of us but recently we lost another one of our ships, the *Vontage*. We thought it was destroyed on a deep-space mission when we lost contact with it after it failed to check in at its scheduled time. Fortunately, they reestablished contact after making repairs to their ship. They found the *Moonslip* and our women had survived."

Shock tore through Dawn. "Seriously? That's great!"

"Yes." Iron didn't look thrilled though. "The *Moonslip* had computer difficulties and crashed into a moon. They were able to shuttle all survivors to a habitable nearby planet that they have lived on since the crash. Our mission is to make repairs to the *Moonslip* and finally take our people home to Garden."

"How many of them survived?"

"All of them but two," he said softly.

"That's amazing that so many are alive. Seriously. To survive a crash and then live on some alien planet. Wow! That had to be rough."

"We are hard to kill and a sturdy breed of adaptors." He turned his head to gaze into her eyes. "I did something that I should have told you about but now it has made my job more difficult."

Stunned, a little afraid too, Dawn studied his eyes. "Okay. What did you do?" For him to think he should have told her about it didn't bode well for good news coming her way.

105

"We recently visited Garden...since I took you. While you were caged. We were only there for a matter of hours before we took this mission. While I was there I made a request of the Cyborg Council. There are twelve of them and they rule our society."

"Okay. What kind of request did you make?" She turned on the bed, her knee against his hip to completely face him so she didn't get a kink in her neck turning her head to stare up at his handsome features.

"I requested to become a family unit with you and it was approved."

No words came to Dawn for long seconds but then a hundred questions filled her mind. "A family what?"

Iron looked grim. "A family unit is exactly like an Earth marriage contract although we call it a family unit since females are rarer on our planet. Cyborg females marry more than one male so that we equally have an opportunity to breed children and have a female in our lives."

Dawn was glad she was sitting down for that bit of news. "How many husbands do the women get, if I'm following what you're saying? And don't think I missed the part about you asking for us to be a family unit. I heard that. I'm just trying to figure out what the hell you did."

"We are under law to have a female take at least three husbands into a family unit but no more than five. They find all the males they wish to breed with. Three is the typical number of males that our females acquire before closing a family unit application."

Dawn was definitely grateful she was sitting down. The information sank in and then she jerked her hand out of his as she nearly leapt off the bed to back away from him in horror as she stared at him. She backed across the room until she bumped into the wall hard enough to flinch as a handle on one of his built-in wall drawers dug into her spine.

A frown instantly curved Iron's lips as he slowly stood. "This is why I didn't wish to tell you what I had done. I didn't think your reaction would be pleasant."

"No fucking way," Dawn hissed. "I didn't agree to some family unit thing. I agreed to be your personal slave. Get me the hell out of that contract. You said it was approved? Rip the damn thing up or get it unapproved or overthrown. Damn you, Iron! How could you do this to me?"

His face noticeably darkened with anger. "You are in a family unit with me and that is final. I didn't need your permission since you're property. There is no getting out of that contract with me, Dawn."

She feared she was going to hyperventilate as her heart started to pound and blood rushed to her ears. She was breathing rapidly as she tried to get a handle on the pure panic that gripped her. Iron closed the distance between them in a few steps and his hands gripped her arms.

"Are you all right? You have gone very pale and I'm alarmed at your reaction."

Dawn struck, kicking the asshole hard with her bare foot to his shin. Pain shot through her toes as she tried to jerk out of his hold. Iron didn't even flinch from the hit but he did tighten his grip on her.

"Calm yourself."

"Fuck you." Hot tears threatened to spill as they filled her eyes. "I trusted you, damn it. I mean, not flat out, all the way, but enough to not screw me this way. How could you?"

107

His fingers eased their tight grip but he didn't release her. He hesitated. "I know this isn't the future you envisioned before I brought you into my life but you need to adjust, Dawn. We are in a family unit and you will come to terms with it. It's done and I am not going to request the contract be reversed. My decision is final."

She let her head drop as she closed her eyes. She didn't want to look into his eyes anymore, feeling betrayed by the bastard. How could he do this? How could he calmly announce he'd signed them up for cyborg's version of marriage? The horror of it was hitting her hard and fast. Tears spilled out of her tightly closed eyelids to spill down her cheeks as her shoulders slumped.

She was trapped, a prisoner, and until she could find a way to escape, she was locked into this hellish nightmare. A sob caught in her throat but she managed to swallow it down. She took some deep breaths, still refusing to look at the man inches in front of her who gripped her arms.

"How many?" Her voice shook.

Iron hesitated. "I estimated that you could handle four."

Bile rose in her throat and her knees collapsed. A bitter laugh escaped her. Iron didn't let her fall, instead he used his hold on her to jerk her against his body. In seconds he adjusted his hands on her and swept her into his arms to carry her to the bed where he gently laid her down. Dawn refused to look at him. She turned away from him as her body settled on the mattress where she curled into a ball, keeping her eyes closed. She hugged her knees.

The silence in the room was absolute. Iron didn't speak and Dawn didn't either. She hugged herself tighter while she fought the urge to flat out bawl. The mockery wasn't lost on her as she tried to muffle another sob. She'd hooked up with Mack all those years ago, gotten her heart smashed, and had plotted her life course to keep from getting involved with another man by working with women. Now she was going to end up married to four of the bastards.

She could live with Iron. She usually liked him. Sometimes she more than liked him, feeling more for him than she wanted to admit. Sometimes right after sex, as she stared into his eyes, her heart squeezed and the thought of losing him was painful. She was falling in love with him, she admitted as she lay there. He, on the other hand, was ready to pass her off to three other men. It spoke volumes to her of how little his emotional attachment to her went. Mack had been a cheating, deceitful bastard, but if another guy even thought about touching her, Mack broke their damn fingers to establish that nobody but him got that privilege.

"I know it is a shock but you will adjust," Iron said softly. His hand brushed her back.

Dawn jerked away from his warm hand. "Don't touch me, damn it. Don't you ever touch me again."

"I will touch you any time that I like." Iron's tone had gone ice cold. "I understand that I am not your ideal mate but you are with me nonetheless." He paused. "I will leave you to let this information settle into your system and we'll discuss it later when you've had an opportunity to calm."

He was fleeing. Anger reared its head as Dawn finally moved. She opened her eyes and turned her head to watch Iron stalk for the door. She knew damn well she shouldn't say a word. At thirty-six-years-old she knew nothing good ever passed her lips in anger but this time she didn't care if she pissed him off.

"Do you know what I'm going to do?"

He stopped walking as the doors slid open. He turned to face her, an angry expression on his handsome features. He said nothing as their gazes locked.

"If you're going to turn me into a whore then I'm going to seduce one of those assholes into kicking your large, sorry ass, Iron. I bet for a blowjob one of your pals you picked to force me to fuck will be more than happy to break your jaw to put that lying mouth of yours out of commission for a while."

Iron stared at her and his silvery skin tone seemed to pale. She nodded at him slowly as she pushed off the bed to give him the dirtiest look she could muster.

"I've haven't gone down on you yet and now I never will but bet on the fact that I will do that for them, Iron. I'm going to have them kicking your sorry ass every damn time I have to suffer one of them touching me so we're both feeling some serious pain."

Iron took a step away from the door and it closed behind him, shutting them both in the small room together. He took another step toward her but Dawn didn't climb on the bed to get away from him. She was too hurt and mad. If he wanted to hit her then she'd hit the son of a bitch back. A punch from him would have hurt less than what he'd done to her by signing her up to fuck other men.

Iron stopped inches in front of her, his blue gaze studying her features carefully. "You thought I meant you could handle four males in a family unit?" He paused. "You're mine, Dawn, and mine alone. My answer of four referred to how many children I think you could safely handle at a future date, to have for me. I would never allow another male to touch you."

Her anger and pain instantly dissipated as quickly as the air left her lungs. She mutely and blankly stared up into his eyes, shocked to the core. Kids? Four of them, with him? Her lips moved but nothing came out. He wasn't going to let three other guys have sex with her. *Nope*, she thought. Iron was talking about his ideal number of kids they could have together. It put a whole new spin on the conversation. She took some deep breaths, trying to get a handle on this new information and finally calmed enough to talk again.

"I never thought I'd be absolutely relieved to hear a guy tell me he wanted four kids with me, but damn am I. Not that I'm agreeing to it," she said quickly, to be clear. "But that's a hell of a lot better than what I thought you were trying to tell me."

"The only male who will touch your body is me, Dawn."

She lifted her hand to place on his chest. The leather texture was thick and she wished it were his skin she touched instead as she continued to gaze up into his eyes. "Okay. Good. I'm not a space hooker and I never want anyone besides you touching me. Are we clear about that?"

"We're in total agreement."

She nodded, her body relaxing. "So tell me what it means to be in a family unit and it better not mean adding more members to our little contract or unit or whatever the hell you call it in cyborg language."

"You're human so you're not obligated under cyborg law to have more than one male in a family unit with you. If you were a cyborg female, you would have no choice. I do not like to share a woman so I decided to form a family unit with you so I never have to allow another male to be with you."

Not the most flattering reason to be married, she decided, but then again, she was relieved that he was the only one she was expected to be with. "That's good to know."

He nodded.

"So why is your job more difficult since you signed up to be married?" She let her hand drop and inched away from him to sit down. Conversations with Iron went better when she was seated since he had a tendency to shock her often. "What's the problem? You said it made your job harder."

Iron hesitated before he took a seat on the edge of the bed a few feet from her. He stared at her as he turned to face her. "There was a female cyborg on Earth that I grew close to during training."

Dread hit Dawn. "A cyborg woman you were with?" She hated the jealousy that struck her but the green monster instantly rose to claw at her gut. "She's one of the survivors?"

Iron nodded in one short movement. "We have the same coloring and we are not a DNA match from the same donors."

"She is a redhead," Dawn guessed aloud. The nasty green monster roared louder in Dawn, knowing damn well that Iron had chosen her off that shuttle because of her coloring. He'd admitted as much to her. "Did you sleep with her on Earth?"

He hesitated, answering Dawn's question without words. She definitely was experiencing hard-core, gut-twisting jealousy at that moment. Her hands fisted and she shoved them into her lap, trying to hide her reaction. There was a woman that Iron had been intimate with that he was now obviously going to be around.

"It was a long time ago," he said softly. "When she saw me yesterday on the planet's surface, she was eager to offer me a family unit contract."

"You're already taken." Dawn was suddenly glad that he'd gone behind her back and married them according to cyborg law. "Did you tell her that?"

Iron gazed into her eyes for long seconds. "I did but she doesn't count it as binding since you're merely human. She has refused to stop trying to pressure me into joining a contract with her. There were very few males on the *Moonslip* since we loaded as many females aboard as possible. With their limited numbers many of the females have been very eager to form family units immediately with our males who arrived in the *Star* and the *Rally*." He paused. "Steel, the commander of the Vontage, was having the same difficulty with the rescued females approaching his males, some of whom are already contracted with females on Garden."

She studied his face, letting her gaze lower down his body to take in his perfectly hot physique with his broad shoulders, muscular arms, and she knew the guy was hung. Iron was any horny woman's wet dream come true in the flesh and then some. At the thought of another woman going after him, possessiveness hit Dawn hard and fast. He was her cyborg. Her name was on his body just as his name was on hers. If that wasn't commitment, she didn't know what was. It was just as good as a marriage ring.

Dawn let that information sink in. "In other words, they haven't been laid in a long time and she's after you like frosting on cake."

"Frosting on cake?" His confused look was comical.

Dawn laughed. "Didn't you ever have a birthday cake? My mother always smeared frosting on it so much the damn thing would collapse under the weight so we were eating mostly frosting. It's a saying."

"I was never given cake. Our birthdays are not celebrated."

Sadness filtered through Dawn. She stood, walked the three feet that separated them then hesitated in front of him to gaze into his beautiful blue eyes.

"I'm sorry. You should celebrate your birthday. Do you know the date you were born?"

"I told you before, I wasn't born. I was grown in a laboratory but I'm aware of my activate date where they allowed me to become conscious for the first time."

She wanted to cry for the things he'd missed, all of it going through her mind. He'd never had overprotective parents to drive him nuts with their smothering love. He didn't have memories of birthdays or Christmas mornings. She hurt for him and it explained how different they were. His cold façade wasn't because he couldn't feel. She'd seen emotions, mostly anger and passion, come from him but he'd never had the platform to express much joy.

"Take your hair down for me."

"I do not take my cleansing here. I do it in my sleeping quarters."

Dawn lowered herself to her knees, using her hands to push his thighs apart to give her room. Her hands slid up his leather-clad thighs to his belt as she went to work to remove it. She dropped it on the floor and her fingers worked the front of his pants next to open them up.

"You wish to have sex with me?"

"Take your hair down for me, baby. I'll reward you if you do."

He frowned. "As much as I enjoy the sex, I refuse to be ordered around, Dawn."

Ignoring his words, she opened his pants. Iron even lifted his hips as she backed out from between his legs to jerk his pants down his hips, down his thighs, and after quickly removing his boots and socks, she dropped his pants on the floor next to them. Her body instantly responded to Iron's aroused cock, standing straight up between his muscular thighs.

"Take off your shirt...please." She knew he was sensitive to being given orders. Her hands gripped his thighs, pushing them wider apart as she moved between them. "And take down your hair if you want me to finish what I start."

Iron frowned at her but he removed his shirt, stripping it off as Dawn watched, so he was totally naked on the edge of the bed. He dropped the shirt and offered her his hand to help her up on the bed with him. A grin spread on her lips as she reached out and put one of hers on his chest instead, trying to push him back but he tensed, not moving the way she wanted him to.

Her attention lowered to his hip and a smile played at her lips as she studied her name in black ink on his beautiful skin next to his hipbone. It did something to her, made her feel things like possessiveness and pride, to see it there on him. Iron was her man. His stiff cock twitched, shifting her focus on it.

"You're going to like this," she said a second before her other hand wrapped around the base of his cock. Her head lowered as Dawn licked her lips. "Damn, are you big, baby. I hope you fit."

"What—"

Dawn licked the crown before her lips wrapped around Iron's cock. She smiled around it as his word turned into a gasp of surprise. Whatever he'd been about to say was probably lost forever. She tested how much of him she could take, knowing damn well she'd never get all of his generous size too deeply into her mouth. Her hand pushed against his chest again but this time he didn't resist lying back for her.

His fingers slid into her hair at the side of her head, caressing her scalp as she worked on him with her mouth, knowing from the way his breathing changed from normal to soft gasps and groans that he was enjoying what she was doing to him.

The taste of him surprised her. Not one to normally enjoy the male taste, she was in for a treat, literally. His pre-cum was sweet instead of bitter tasting. She moaned around his stiff length, her tongue teasing the underside of his cock as she sucked. She lifted up to almost totally remove it from her mouth so she could swirl her tongue around the ridged crown, her tongue exploring every little aspect of him.

The fingers in her hair tightened. "Don't stop, Dawn." His tone was gruff.

She released him completely with her mouth to look up the length of his body, loving how incredibly sexy he looked lying across the bed, his stomach muscles tight, showing every defined groove there.

"Undo your hair for me and I won't."

Iron lifted his head to look down his body to glower at her. "Are you serious?"

She licked her lips, making a show of it. Easing down, she opened her mouth and licked him slowly from the underside over the rounded tip of his aroused flesh. She paused. "Unbind your hair, Iron."

He growled but he released her hair to reach up to his own. He had to shift a little but she saw him tearing at the ties that bound the bottom of his long braid. Smiling, she went back to his cock, opening her mouth to take him back inside. The taste of pre-cum was definitely sweet and delicious. She wondered how he'd taste when he came and decided to find out.

His cock was thick and the head was mushroom-shaped enough that the rim was a noticeable sensation on her tongue. She turned her head, going at him from a newer angle, and took him deeper into the back of her mouth. The hand returned to her hair, his fingers gripping a fistful of hair but he didn't pull it or try to lead her movements. His breathing picked up again to a near pant as she moved up and down on him, turning her head over and over, feeling her tongue rasp on his skin as she took him a little deeper still.

His hips rose from the bed as his thighs tensed, letting Dawn know he was damn close. She sucked harder on him, moving faster, and Iron rasped her name a second before he started coming inside her mouth. The sweet flavor of him filled her as she swallowed his release down, enjoying every groan he made as he kept coming. His body jerked, almost choking her as he pushed deeper into her mouth so she eased back an inch, suckling him until his hips dropped back to the bed and his legs relaxed.

Dawn gently eased his cock from her between her lips, taking a few swipes at it with her tongue before she completely lifted her head. Her gaze rose. Iron's hair was free, spilling across the cover of his bed, his head turned to the side, his eyes closed. She got up from her knees to strip out of her clothes, never taking her attention away from him.

Iron turned his head and his gaze fixed on her. He was so handsome with his hair free, the blue of his eyes really startling against his light silvery skin with that fiery red mass of long curly hair spread out around him. His features were relaxed in a satisfied and wholly pleased way, making him look a little vulnerable with his guard obviously down. Naked, she climbed onto the bed next to him to stretch out on her side. Her fingers went into his glorious hair, instantly loving how the bright curls wrapped around her hand as she gripped it.

"I love your hair."

Full lips curved downward into an unhappy look. "That was blackmail."

She grinned. "It was and it worked. Your hair is gorgeous. Why do you always keep it braided? What is the point of having it down to your ass if you keep it tied up?"

"It reminds me I am free." He paused. "When I was on Earth they kept us shaved bald. It is my way of rebelling."

"I'm glad then that you're a rebel because I want to rub your hair across my body. It's so sexy."

A red eyebrow arched. "What is the point of that?"

Grinning, Dawn took a handful of his hair and rubbed it over his nipple. It responded instantly, hardening into a stiff point. Her gaze lifted to his. She wiggled her eyebrows.

Iron suddenly rolled them over, pinning her down. "You will pay for that."

Chapter Eight

"I can't wait." Dawn grinned, not feeling fear at all. "Are you going to tie me up and fuck me?"

His beautiful dark blue eyes widened slightly with surprise. "You'd enjoy that?"

"I would," she admitted softly. She played with his hair that fell over his shoulders, her hands not able to touch it enough. "You're so damn sexy, Iron. Have I mentioned that to you?"

He tilted his head to stare down at her with a frown. "I believe you mean it."

"You don't need to look so happy about it."

"I'm not happy."

"Have you ever heard of sarcasm, baby?"

"Why do you call me that?"

"Baby?" Dawn shifted her legs, wrapping them around the back of his thighs where he had her pinned flat under him. "Does it bother you?"

"I'm not a child."

"It's a sweet nickname. It beats me calling you other names, doesn't it?"

"You could call me Iron."

"I could call you asshole too. Don't push your luck."

His frown deepened. Dawn sighed.

"What's wrong with me calling you baby sometimes? It's not an insult. It's something I say when I'm feeling close to you. What's your problem?"

"I don't like it."

Taking a deep breath, she expelled the air from her lungs. "Fine. I won't call you that anymore."

She untangled her fingers from his hair and reached up under his arms so she could put her arms around his waist. She smiled as she let her hands slide down and fill with beefy muscled ass. She loved touching him. Iron's eyes widened as she massaged his ass cheeks.

"What are you doing now?"

"I'm enjoying the feel of your ass." She shifted her hips, feeling the hard press of his cock against her thigh. "I'm so wet from going down on you. Either fuck me or play with me. I don't care if you use your mouth or your fingers but I need you to touch me."

Iron pushed up and slowly slid down her body, forcing her to release her grip on his ass. Dawn smiled as his hair trailed along her sides, tickling her in the best way. She spread her thighs as her heart sped up. She loved him going down her body and the light kisses he brushed along the way had her clit throbbing with need to be touched by the time his lips finally reached her inner thigh, inches from the place she ached.

He turned his head a little and his fingers spread her sex lips apart. Dawn stretched her thighs as wide as possible and bent her knees up out of his way as she reached down to touch his hair that was across both sides of her thighs. It was a sensual thing to have his long tresses teasing her flesh as he started to lick her clit with the tip of his tongue.

121

"That feels amazing," she whispered, bowing her back so her hips tilted to offer him better access. "I'm so turned-on."

Iron's full lips encircled her swollen nub as he started to gently suck, the flat of his tongue going to work on her. Bliss poured through Dawn at his intimate kiss, drawing her closer to climax. Her body tensed and her vaginal walls tightened as his tongue moved faster, rubbing against her in a way that had her panting and moaning loudly. Her fingers released his hair so she didn't pull it, grabbing for the bedding next to her hips instead, to claw at it.

His hand shifted and a finger slowly entered her pussy to push in deep, coaxing a louder moan from her. She moved her hips slowly and almost cried out in protest when that finger withdrew but before she could, he pushed in two digits, the feeling of him stretching her, pushing in deep as he started to finger fuck her to the pace his tongue set. Dawn tossed her head, arched her back, and cried out his name as pleasure slammed through her as she came.

His mouth left her clit with one last tug and his fingers withdrew. His hair caressed her body as he lifted up, the mattress shifting with his weight as he inched up her body enough that he hovered just over her. Dawn opened her eyes to stare into his passion-filled gaze.

He braced his upper body with one hand and reached between them, grabbing his hard cock to steer it right where she wanted him. The crown of his sex slid through her wet slit twice before he positioned himself right at the entrance of her pussy. With a shift of his hips he entered her with one strong thrust.

Dawn cried out in pleasure as he filled her an inch at a time. Her hands released the bedding to grab onto his shoulders, her palms sliding over the tattoos across the tops of his shoulders to his back, pulling him down on her as he settled his chest against hers. She loved having his weight pin her, his sheer size making her feel petite and feminine as he adjusted until he was bracing his body with his elbows. Their gazes remained locked as he started to move.

She wrapped her legs high on his waist, her heels digging into his ass where she could feel muscles flexing as he picked up the speed of his driving hips. She didn't look away from his gaze as he powered into her, making her feel passion reignite with every movement he made. They moved together, building the desire they shared until her body tensed in promise of another mind-blowing orgasm.

Iron shifted his hips more, lifting up a little to drive downward inside her body. With every movement the shaft of his cock rubbed against her swollen and already oversensitive clit—from what his mouth had done to her minutes earlier. The overload of intense stimulation of her sex was too much to take anymore. There was no holding back as she started to buck under him, ecstasy tearing through her from her pussy straight to her brain. Dawn threw her head back, her eyes closing, and she cried out Iron's name, feeling her inner muscles quiver and shake with the force of how hard she was coming.

"Dawn," Iron groaned, his head falling forward to drop against her shoulder. His hips jerked in sharp movements.

Holding him tightly until he stilled after his own release tore through him was heaven to Dawn. The sex between them was incredible and

123

intense. Pure satisfaction held her in its grip, such a warm and wonderful sensation that she wished she could freeze the moment in time forever to keep. She loved being under him, wrapped around his body, to be a part of him while they were still physically joined. She turned her head enough so they were cheek to cheek as they caught their breath.

He's mine, Dawn thought. *He carries my name on his body like I carry his. He married us according to cyborg law.* She had always been afraid to commit, afraid of getting hurt again but she had to admit to herself as she clung to Iron that she didn't hate the thought of staying with him. It stunned her as she lay there to realize that the last thing she wanted was to escape.

Iron nuzzled her, his lips brushing the top of her shoulder. "I like seeing my brand on you."

His breath tickled a little but then the tip of his tongue slid on her skin as he brushed it against her, and then he turned his face into her neck, just lying on her, holding her. He didn't move off or try to separate them, seemingly content to just stay as they were. She was grateful for it.

"Iron?"

"Am I crushing you?" He started to lift up off her.

Dawn clung to him. "Don't move. Please? Just stay this way."

He relaxed on her, settling back to the way he'd been. "This is pleasant. Are you sure you I'm not too heavy?"

"I'm sure." She hesitated. "Since we're married, will you please sleep with me now?"

His body barely tensed but it was noticeable. "I don't believe that would be a good idea."

Sadness filled her instantly. "You still think I'm going to try to hurt you?"

He hesitated. "I don't fully trust you yet."

She turned her head away. *Great*, she thought, *I'm married to a guy who won't share a bed with me while he's asleep and vulnerable.* "What do you think I'm going to do?"

"If I were in your place, I would try to coax my captor into believing I was docile and then escape the first chance opportunity arose."

"I'm not you." She paused. "I'm still stunned we're married but I don't hate the concept as much as I thought I would now that I know it means that it's just us in this relationship."

Iron's head lifted and she knew he was staring at her. She turned her head to meet his gaze. He studied her features closely for a good minute.

"You don't look pleased with it either."

"I'm married to a man who won't sleep with me. If I wanted to escape, I wouldn't do it while you were sleeping next to me. This bed is so small we're going to be plastered together so you would wake up if I tried to get out of bed. Isn't it smarter if you watch me every chance you get if you're so worried about that? Hell, you being gone so much gives me more opportunities if I wanted to bust out of this room."

He nodded. "True, but if I keep my distance from you then when you attempt it I won't take it as personally as I would if I let you spend more time with me."

His honesty stunned her. "So that's your big plan? You want to have four kids with me at some point but you're going to keep us emotionally distanced?"

"That is the plan."

"Your plan sucks." Anger started to burn inside her. "I don't want that kind of marriage. If we're going to do this, then don't be half-assed about it, Iron. You either want a wife or a sex slave."

"I have both."

"Damn it," she hissed. She pushed at his chest. "Get up."

He withdrew from her body as he eased his weight off, pushing up with his arms to get on his knees on the bed. Dawn scooted back to sit up and glare at him the second she was free. She went to her knees, to face him.

"Do I have to kick your ass to get you to treat me right?"

"You couldn't beat me in a fight."

"Piss me off enough and you might be surprised." She walked on her knees until she was inches from him. His body tensed but he didn't move back to put more space between them. "You said we're married so we might as well give it a shot."

He just stared down at her.

"Damn it, Iron." She reached up to place one hand on his chest while her other hand reached for a long lock of his hair that had fallen over his shoulder. She really loved his hair, she decided, as her fingers played with the soft texture of it before she lifted her gaze to his. "Let's use your wonderful logic then."

"There's no logical reason why I should sleep in the same bed with you. I don't know why you insist upon it. The bed is too small to share comfortably and logically you should appreciate not having to share small quarters with a roommate."

"Okay, so logic is out. I want to sleep with you. I want to feel your skin against mine when I go to sleep and wake up. I want to use the cleansing unit with you and wash your back for you. I want you to wash mine. We're having sex and we should be more intimate in other ways. It might not be the smartest thing to do but I want it all the same."

"The cleansing foam washes our bodies so I don't need assistance."

Frustration flared. "Damn, Iron. You're killing me here. Washing each other's backs isn't because of a damn need to get cleaner. Have you ever shared a shower with someone?"

He shook his head. "No."

Dawn released his hair and inched away from him, backing off the bed. She stared at him as she stood. "Come here."

Iron only hesitated for a second before he moved to meet her. Dawn turned and went to the cleansing unit. She stepped over the rim on the floor and motioned him to follow.

"It's too small to fit both of us."

"Get in here, damn it." She hesitated. "Please? I want to show you something."

He sighed, not looking amused one bit, but to her surprise, he did what she demanded, though she had expected him to refuse. She hit the button and the wall rose to close them inside. It was a tight fit but she didn't mind being pressed to his side. She activated the foam, closing her eyes as it sprayed down on them. The tingling sensation was instant as it coated her skin. The second the foam stopped spraying she reached up and wiped it off her face, opened her eyes to watch Iron wipe it from his face. Their gazes met.

Dawn pushed him against the wall, invading what little space he had. One of her hands slid between his thighs to cup his balls. The foam was slippery and warm. She watched his face, feeling amusement as he hissed out a sharp breath.

"Relax. I'm cleaning you," she teased as her hand massaged him and her fingernails gently raked sensitive skin between his anus and sac. "Tell me when you see the point of sharing a cleansing unit."

Her other hand wrapped around his hardening cock. She explored, making him harder as blood rushed there along with desire that flared in his eyes. Dawn knew she had him as her own body came alive while the foam worked, cleaning their skin, causing those little tingles that had to be adding to the pleasure Iron was feeling as she worked him with her hands.

Iron groaned softly as his breathing increased. The foam started to melt and turn to liquid. Dawn leaned in as she fixed her attention on his nipple, closed her mouth over it and nibbled on him. Her lips encased his areola as she started to suck, rubbing her bottom teeth over the hardening tip. She smiled as one of his hands gripped her ass, his other hand slid between her legs, which she parted for him, so he could tease the inside of her thighs. He dragged her closer so it made it difficult for her to pump his cock slowly since his erection was now pressed to her belly. Another deep groan tore from his throat, louder than the first one.

Adjusting her hold on him she used her stomach to rub the underside of his jutting cock with her hand holding him firmly in place on the topside. She moved her body against his, rubbing up and down him just as a cat would against a scratching post. She released his nipple to go for the other one.

His hand left her ass to slide up the curve of her spine until he reached her neck. Firm fingers gripped her hair, tugging until she was left with no choice but to feel pain or release him with her mouth. She opened her mouth and tipped her head back to stare into his intense gaze.

Iron lowered his face, his mouth taking possession of hers in a heartbeat. She moaned against his tongue that brushed against hers as his finger rubbed slow circles around her swelling clit. Her hand lifted from his balls to grip the top of his shoulder and she released his cock to grab his other shoulder. She lifted a leg high, bending her knee to wrap around the back of his thigh as she pushed off with her other leg. She left him no choice but to lift her as she climbed his taller frame.

Breaking the kiss, she stared into his passion-filled gaze, now level with hers. "Fuck me here. Right now."

Another groan tore from Iron but his hands shifted on her, cupping her ass as he took a step forward until her back pressed against the wall. He shifted his hips, lifting her higher, and then he pressed against her as he slowly sank into her welcoming depths. She was wet and ready to take him, so turned-on she knew she should be shocked at her responses to him. Instead she enjoyed the sensation of being filled by him as he lowered her until he was tightly encased in her pussy.

Iron took her mouth again, kissing her as he slowly started to move inside her. Dawn clung to his shoulders, her legs locking around his slippery, wet hips. He lifted and pulled her body up and down instead of thrusting his hips. His sheer strength made her hotter. She'd never had sex standing up before but she loved the sensation of the smooth wall rubbing her back and how all she had to do was cling to him.

She twisted her hips as he moved her faster. She had to break from the kiss, unable to stop herself from turning her head and going for the skin on his neck instead. She licked at the water there and then opened her mouth, gently nipping him with her teeth. The response it drew from Iron was instant as he pressed her body more firmly against the wall, pinning her there, holding her still as he started to move his hips instead of her. He drove up into her fast and hard, out of control, just the way she liked him. Their breathing increased to loud panting as Iron fucked her harder and deeper against the wall, powering into her over and over, creating a wonderful friction that had her burning with hot desire, her vaginal muscles tensing and clamping around him as the rapture built. She could only feel and enjoy their bodies moving against each other, his chest rubbing her nipples until they were swollen and so sensitive she wanted to scream from the unbearable pleasure.

Iron lowered his face and his teeth sank into her shoulder. The bite he gave her sent a shaft of pain splintering through her body and threw her into overload of sensation. A scream burst from her as she came hard. Pleasure and pain blurred into oblivion as ecstasy ripped through her very soul. Iron tore his mouth from her skin and threw his head back, shouting out as he came, his cock throbbing hard inside her against her quivering muscles as he shot his release into her body.

Dawn was slumped against his chest, her face pressed against his shoulder, her arms wrapped around his neck when she came out of her haze of sexual gratification. Her shoulder throbbed a little but it was nothing compared to the warmth and sensitivity coming from her lower region as Iron gently withdrew from her pussy. One arm was wrapped around her waist, holding her tightly against him and his other hand was still clamped on the curve of her ass. Her legs shook as she tried to unwrap them from his waist. He slowly lowered her on her shaky legs until she was standing in the cleansing unit again. She looked up at him and saw remorse.

"I'm sorry."

"For what?"

His hand released her ass and he stepped back, keeping his arm loosely around her waist to steady her. "I was rough with you and I left teeth marks." His attention focused on her throbbing shoulder. "I don't know why I bit you. The skin isn't broken but you will probably have a bruise there."

A chuckle came from Dawn. "I bit you first."

His frown deepened, lining his mouth with tiny little wrinkles. "I enjoyed your teeth. I think that is why I bit you back but I shouldn't have. I do apologize."

Shaking her head, Dawn grinned at him. "Do you know how intense that was? The second your teeth clamped down...oh fuck, baby. I guess I'm twisted because it totally got me off. Don't look so glum. I liked it."

He looked anything but happy. "You said you wouldn't call me that anymore."

"Fine." She grinned though. "How about 'stud muffin'?" She ran her hand from his stomach to his chest, enjoying the feel of his warm, firm skin under her fingertips and palm. "Or 'beef cakes'?" Her grin widened at his horrified look. "'Love cookie' that I want to eat?"

Iron's expression shut down, his features going blank. He released her, his arm shooting to the side so his hand hit the button. The wall behind him slid down, opening up the cleansing unit. Iron spun on his heel and stepped over the rim, stalking into the room, toward the bed. Dawn enjoyed teasing him. She stepped over the rim to get out. He needed to lighten the hell up.

"How about 'frosting'? I enjoy licking you."

She nearly slammed into him when Iron suddenly spun around. The anger she saw on his features stunned her and her grin died as she stared up into his darkening face. His teeth clenched and the muscles of his jaw were visible from the action. Two hands gripped her in an instant but he didn't hurt her as they clamped on her upper arms.

"Why are you making fun of me?"

Surprise and disbelief at how he'd taken her teasing left her speechless.

"I know that you must dislike me for stealing you off the shuttle but at least let me get dressed before you taunt me."

"Iron—"

He cut her off. "I let my guard down during intercourse with you, believing it was the one time that you would accept me."

132

"Iron—"

He gave her a gentle push as he released her. He stepped away, gathered his clothes from the floor and dumped them on the bed. He grabbed his pants, not bothering with his briefs and bent to put them on. He lifted a leg and Dawn struck, throwing herself at him to hit him in the ass with her body.

Iron gasped as he was pushed forward onto the bed. Dawn didn't hesitate to use his surprise to topple over on him, her body landing on his. He grabbed her and they rolled as he tried to get her off him. The small bed wasn't wide enough for the move and Dawn met air instead of mattress as he rolled them. She knew it was coming in a panicked second but there was no stopping it as she slammed onto the floor with two-hundred-fifty-plus-pounds of wet, pissed-off cyborg male falling on top of her.

The air was knocked from her lungs. She was stunned and pain shot up her back. The weight shifted on her and she heard Iron cursing loudly as he lifted off her enough for her to gasp in air. Her eyes flew open to see Iron's face hovering inches over hers, concern showing in those beautiful eyes.

"Are you all right? I didn't mean for that to happen. Speak to me. Tell me if you need a medic. Why the hell did you attack me? I reacted without being able to stop myself. I'm sorry, Dawn."

She took another breath, pretty sure the pain in her back was fading and that no major damage had been done. It wasn't as if he'd hit her, which would have definitely caused damage. Nope. They'd only fallen off the bed and he'd landed on her. He was a big guy and heavy. Her hands shook as she reached up. She half expected him to grab her wrists to stop her, knowing damn well he had reflexes that fast but he let her cup his face with her hands.

"I wasn't making fun of you or mocking you." She licked her lips, wetting them. "Nor was I taunting you. I call you baby as an endearment. Since you don't like that one, I was trying to find one you'd like and I was trying to make you laugh. You tend to take things way too seriously. I was amused, sure, but it wasn't in a mean way. I want to call you something sweet."

He searched her eyes, probably trying to judge if she were telling him the truth. She stared back at him and didn't look away or try to hide her feelings from him. Her hands caressed his jawline and cheeks. His tense body relaxed a little. She saw regret flash in his eyes before he slowly nodded.

"I believe you. Did I hurt you when I landed on you?"

"I think I'm good." She wasn't about to mention that she was sure her tailbone was bruised. It throbbed and ached but she would rather suffer a little pain than risk making him feel worse. "I want to call you something besides Iron when we're intimate."

"Why?"

She hesitated, trying to think of an explanation he could relate to. "Anyone can call you Iron but I'm not just anyone. I'm yours and you're mine. I want a nickname to give you that no one else can call you."

"It's a strange human custom, isn't it?" He looked irritated.

"Yes." She smiled. "It is."

He lifted a little more off her body as he eased away from her and got to his feet. He bent down to help her up. Dawn managed to hide the wince she stifled as her back protested being upright. Iron steered her around and then, to her surprise, he crouched behind her. His breath fanned on the curve of her ass as his fingertips brushed her back.

"You have red marks from the floor."

"I'm good." She turned her head to peer at him over her shoulder. "Nothing is broken."

Iron straightened to his full height and turned her to face him. "Do not attack me like that again, Dawn. Sometimes it is instinct that takes over before I can stop myself when I'm not expecting you to do those kinds of things. Do you understand? Luckily I just rolled to get you off me but I could have struck out with my fist. I never want to accidentally harm you."

"I wasn't attacking you. I was tackling your ass to make you listen to me before you could storm out of here thinking I was being a mean bitch. You're way too paranoid."

"What am I going to do with you?" His tone was soft, almost a whisper.

"Sleep with me to make it up to me that you landed on me like a house?"

A small smile played at his lips. "No."

"I could have a concussion." She smiled as she said it to let him know she was teasing. "You're supposed to wake the injured party every hour." She winked at him. "We could fool around."

"It wouldn't be the intelligent or logical thing to do."

"Welcome to my world. I rarely do what I know I should but sometimes it all turns out all right."

An eyebrow rose. "Give me an example."

Dawn lifted her hands, curving them around his hips. "You."

"What about me?"

"I know I shouldn't want you. You kidnapped me and brought me here against my will, tricked me into agreeing to be your sex slave but…" She pressed against his body, staring into his eyes. "I do want you. I want you to sleep with me so I can enjoy how you make me feel when I'm in your arms. I really love it when you hold me. I could have killed you the day you brought me in here but I didn't. I wouldn't," she said softly. "I know it's stupid, but damn, I enjoy spending time with you even when you drive me nuts with the way you like to keep your distance from me."

"You are little and you can't harm me, Dawn."

As she stared up at him, she realized he was always going to be suspicious of her. "I'm a mechanic, Iron. You know that."

He nodded. "What does that have to do with anything?"

She hesitated. He would either finally realize she meant him no harm or he'd tie her ass to the bed forever. "You made mistakes, like leaving the cleansing unit on for my use. If you lift the grid plate along the left side of the wall next to it, you'll find active wires to give it power."

She paused. She didn't look away from him as she said words that would either get him to finally believe her or he'd be even more suspicious. It was a risk but she wanted him to trust her. It had become important to her. He was becoming important to her.

"There's about five feet of surplus cable, just enough to go under the floor plates to hook anywhere I wanted to on the metal grates that vent the room with fresh air. I could have hooked live wires to the plate by the dresser where you walk every time you get out of bed with me to dress. You never would have known what hit you and you never use the cleanser in here so you wouldn't have had a clue I'd disabled it. The energy level is enough to kill you if I tear out the regulator sensor which is accessible in that panel. It would have been easy to fry your ass if I wanted you dead."

Iron stared at her mutely for long seconds, his grim expression telling her that he wasn't happy with what she'd said. He jerked out of her hold, went the wall and then tore the plate off that she'd mentioned. He studied it for a good minute before he turned back to her. The plate in his hand dropped, clattering loudly to the floor. The look in his eyes told her he knew she was right and he'd verified with his own eyes that it was possible to do.

"Why didn't you do it?" His voice was soft.

"The last thing I want is to hurt you, Iron."

He took a deep breath. "I'll sleep here tonight. We'll try it."

Chapter Nine

Dawn woke to the hard press of one very aroused male doing a heartbeat impression against her ass and thigh where his cock was tucked downward. The room was dark, the lights still off in sleep cycle, and a sexy male was pressed firmly against her back. The arm around her waist was heavy but she enjoyed the weight pinning her. Her cheek rested on Iron's bicep, the best damn pillow she'd ever slept on. He was warm, big, and she enjoyed waking up to him.

He was still in bed with her. Her lips curved in a wide smile. Waking up to Iron in bed with her was a terrific experience and one she'd wondered about often. Now that she knew how good it was she was determined to make him sleep with her every night. She wiggled her ass against his cock while the arm tightened around her waist. His hand moved to cup her breast, his palm rubbing her soft flesh.

"Morning, baby."

"I don't like that one," he rumbled at her.

"Stud muffin?"

He sighed. "You start this the moment you wake up?"

"I want to give you a special nickname I can use when we're having sex or we're about to have it." She wiggled her ass against him again and chuckled as his cock jerked in response. "And soon."

"Fine. I didn't mind it when you called me sexy but never call me that in public or around other persons. Am I clear?"

"Perfectly, sexy." She enjoyed the sound of it rolling off her tongue.

"I suppose you expect me to call you a special nickname?"

Surprise flashed through and her heart rate increased, pleased that he'd think of that. "It would be nice."

His thumb and forefinger pinched her nipple gently and rolled the tip of her breast between both digits. He gave the flesh he gripped a tiny tug as he shifted his knee, pressing it between her thighs. She spread them to make room for him. His leg slid up until he applied pressure between the vee of her thighs, his skin rubbing against her clit. Dawn softly moaned.

"I really like sleeping with you and waking up like this."

"I am seeing the benefit." He paused. "Sleeping with someone was pleasant. I was certain I would be unable to relax but I slept well."

He sounded a little surprised and it gave her a thought. "You've never shared a bed with someone while sleeping before?"

"No."

She lifted her leg more, spreading her thighs. "Never?"

"I just said I had not."

"What about the cyborg you used to have sex with? You didn't sleep with her?"

He stopped playing with her nipple, released it. "No. They kept us in separate cell units. We were only able to have intercourse on the shuttle we flew to pick up supplies while we were on shift. There was no sleeping involved and the sex was always rushed due to time constraints. We were…" He paused. "Experimenting."

"What about after you were free?"

"I had intercourse with plenty of women but I never stayed over. There was no reason to. We had our own quarters, we shared sex, and then I left."

Dawn didn't enjoy the idea of Iron being with anyone else but it soothed her some to know she was the only woman he'd held in his arms while he slumbered. It turned her on more, knowing that. She rubbed against his thigh, another moan coming from her parted lips.

"Fuck me, sexy."

Iron nuzzled her neck with his jaw. "Roll on your stomach and spread your thighs."

She hesitated and then followed his orders. The bed was narrow so she had to wait for him to lift up from the bed to give her room to spread her thighs wide. She wondered if he was going to give her a back massage with her flat on her stomach but then, to her shock, he came down on top of her, crushing her flat under him.

She would have asked what he was doing but was distracted by the press of his hard cock a second before he entered her pussy in one downward drive of his hips as he settled fully between her legs. She groaned, clawing at the bedding. She'd never had a man take her this way. She'd done it doggy style but had never been pinned completely flat under a man. She realized his weight held her totally immobile and she couldn't even push her ass back against him.

"Tell me if I hurt you," he whispered in her ear as he started to move on her, his thighs spreading to push hers farther apart as he shifted his body a little more over hers.

Iron's hand dug between her hip and the mattress but she was too concentrated on his thick shaft sliding inside her, hitting sensitive nerves that awakened with each deep penetration and slow sliding motion, to realize what he was doing until two of his fingers pressed against her clit. He gently pinched the bud between his fingers and as he moved on her, it tugged the bundle of nerves with every powerful drive in and out of her body.

A keening sound came from her lips between pants. It was intense delight as he fucked her. Dawn couldn't move at all except to claw at the bedding as Iron totally took control of their lovemaking. His breath was hot and heavy on the back of her neck as he used one arm to hold enough of his weight off her so she could pull breath into her lungs. The warmth of his breath tickled her skin. He was strong and his movements on her rubbed the front of her body against the mattress and sheets, his skin sliding along the back of her, and then there were his wonderful fingers and cock engaging her clit and pussy.

"Oh God," she nearly sobbed. "Iron!"

"You can take me," he growled, moving faster on her, riding her hard and deep.

The sound of skin slapping skin was nearly as loud as their choppy breathing. Iron made wonderful little groans as he twisted his hips, coming at her from different angles, making her feel every delicious inch of his amazingly hard cock. The pleasure was more than she thought she could endure but with Iron pinning her down there was no way to make him ease back on the intensity. All she could do was feel the ecstasy building, knowing that he was going to drive her over the edge of sanity and reason with how strong she would come.

The fingers against her clit started to move as he bent them, tapping against her clit as he ground his hips down harder, forcing her to take even more of him as skin pressed tightly against skin. He hit a new level of erogenous zones with the thick crown of his cock, driving her passion higher. Dawn nearly sobbed with the need to come. With the stimulation to her bundled nerves on her exterior and what he was doing to the ones inside her pussy she couldn't think, couldn't form words, drowning in the intensity of all that was Iron.

A scream tore from Dawn as she started climaxing, the sheer intensity of it slamming her so hard she nearly blacked out as it flashed through her in a wave of fiery heat, nearly burning her alive. Her muscles quivered hard, making her shake all over, and behind her Iron buried his face in the crook of her neck, gasping for breath as he kept powering into her, kept coaxing to draw out her release until Dawn fought blacking out.

Iron stilled suddenly, freezing, his fingers releasing her clit as he flattened them on the mattress. His sex throbbed the way a clenching fist would against her interior muscles and he groaned loudly as he started to come, his hot cum filling her. He moved, withdrawing almost totally from her body before slowly sinking back into her, a softer groan coming from his parted lips against her skin as he taunted both of their over-sensitized sexual organs. He shook slightly on top of her, his bigger body quivering. He stilled again.

His lips brushed her neck, placing a feather light kiss there, a second before he took a deep, calming breath.

"I wanted to make it last but you respond too well to me and my intentions are forgotten."

Still panting and out of breath, Dawn forced her eyes open to stare into the dark room. She may as well have been blind because she couldn't make out anything. "I'm not complaining. I like quickies."

"That was quick but I enjoyed it a lot."

"Me too."

He hesitated. "Did I hurt you? I try to be gentle with you but you seem to enjoy it when I am not. The harder I pound into you the wetter you get. You're so hot inside that you make me a little crazy. No one has ever made me lose control the way you do, Dawn."

It was the best compliment he'd ever given her. To break Iron's control was saying a lot. He was a freak about keeping himself in check. She grinned in the darkness, feeling safe that he wouldn't be able to see it.

"I'm great. So, isn't sleeping in bed with me nice? It's definitely got a plus side, doesn't it?"

He was silent for long seconds before he brushed another kiss on her neck, his lips just a soft butterfly tap but she appreciated the sentiment. "I will give up my temporary quarters and we can try to live together on a trial basis but if it doesn't work for me I will return to sleeping in separate quarters."

Dawn had to admit his words made her happy. She was lonely in his room but that wasn't the reason joy surged through her. She wanted to sleep in his arms and she wanted to share a foaming cleansing with him again, but mostly, she just wanted to spend more time with Iron.

Damn, she thought, as her grin faded. She put her cheek on the mattress and fought a few seconds of pure panic. She was falling in love with Iron. It was a mistake and she realized it. She always prided herself on being a realist and they were too different to make it work. She had her life planned out and none of it included being a man's slave, even if he were the best damn lover she'd had and the absolute sexiest man ever created. Literally.

"What is wrong?"

She'd been so lost in her thoughts that she'd nearly forgotten he still pinned her flat under him. She wiggled her ass a tiny bit—all she could do with his heavy weight—but he seemed to understand as he shifted his body on her, his hand sliding out from under her hip so he could brace his hands on the bed on both sides of her. He lifted off and out of her body. Dawn missed him immediately, both his cock inside her and his secure weight that had been on her. The mattress shifted and light blinded her as the motion sensors automatically reacted to Iron getting off the bed by bringing the light to full.

"Dawn? I asked you a question. What is wrong?"

It took a lot for her to turn her head to stare at him where he stood just feet from her. The fact that he was naked and still semi erect was a distraction as her gaze swept slowly upward to his frowning features and dark, narrowed eyes.

"Your breathing changed and your eyes look..." He paused, cocking his head just slightly to study her gaze. "You look sad. Did I harm you?"

She shook her head. "I promise you didn't hurt me. I might be feeling you for a few hours but it's all in the best way."

"Feeling me?" His eyebrows shot up.

"It's a saying." She couldn't stop the grin that hit her. "I am going to be a bit tender but you didn't hurt me. I was just thinking how different we are. That's all. It makes me wonder how we're going to work things out." She did want to make things work, she silently acknowledged.

"You do what I say, follow my orders, and we will have no issues to have conflict over."

"Really?" She had to hold back the urge to snort. "Is that all?"

He nodded. His long hair was gorgeous and she hated that her attention went to it. The urge to go to her knees, inch toward him, and run her fingers through the long strands was almost impossible to resist. It was just wrong that he was that beautiful and kissable all at once. It was hard to be angry at the silver-skinned, luscious specimen of masculinity.

"We should get in the cleansing unit," she said suddenly, pulling her attention from staring at him. She was afraid she'd crawl toward him to pull him back into bed. No man had ever affected her the way he did, making her almost a sex-starved woman. She'd just had sex with him but damned if she didn't want a repeat. "Yeah. Definitely a foaming down is in order."

"I overslept," he turned, bending for his clothing. "I have to get to work or I will be late. I will cleanse after my shift."

She glanced at the clock on the wall, seeing the time, and then looked back at him to openly gawk at his fine ass displayed just feet from her as he jerked up his pants. He straightened, both of his hands going for his hair.

145

She watched mutely as he finger combed the wild, long strands, parting them into three sections at the back of his head, and proceeded to braid it.

"You don't need a mirror to see what you're doing?"

He turned, his fingers still working his hair into a long rope. "No. I don't own one."

She nodded. "I noticed. I just assumed you'd removed it so I couldn't break it to use for a weapon."

"I never put one in. I have done this for a very long time."

It was a reminder that he was about her father's age. She swallowed that down, focused instead on his muscular, fine chest. He sure didn't look older than his mid-thirties. He was the fittest male she'd ever had the pleasure of drooling over. She swallowed and got off the bed.

"So I guess I won't get breakfast if you're in a sure-fire rush."

His hands stilled. "I will have someone bring you food. Just do not allow them to come inside the room and do not," his eyes narrowed, "try to run. I will have two males bring your food in case you implement a plan to attack one."

"What is on your agenda today?" She let his comment go.

Iron found the tie to his hair on the floor, bending down to sweep it up, and tied off the end of his braid to secure it. He eyed her for a long second and then reached for his shirt. "I have to go to the planet surface to work on their shuttle. Shuttles are my specialty since I'm able to link with the computer on board directly."

"She can talk to you."

He hesitated. "In a way, yes."

"That must be cool. I sure wish the station computer could have talked to me when I was working on her. I heard about those neat abilities but after the cyborg project failed, they outlawed having those kind of implants installed in our brains."

"That is good," Iron said softly. "There are side effects that come with them."

Curiosity reared its head in Dawn. "What kinds?"

He paused as he buttoned his uniform shirt. "Occasionally, if I use my transmitter too often, I will get nose bleeds or slight headaches. It is from the vibrations of it being active for long periods of time. There is no long-term damage or threat but it can be annoying. Of course I was designed to heal faster and be more resilient than you are. I don't know what the long-term effects would have on a full human."

"I wish I could go with you," she said softly. "Do you know what I'd give to get my hands on something to do?"

Iron finished dressing, his gaze lifting to hers where he held it for a long moment. "There is nowhere to escape on the planet's surface. It is a dangerous environment."

"Get over the whole 'trying to escape' thing. I told you I wasn't going to do that, damn it."

His gaze was direct as he studied her. "Get dressed quickly."

Shock tore through Dawn as her knees went weak. Hope and excitement lit a fire inside her. "You'll let me go with you? Really?"

His hesitation was only a few seconds long. "You behaved well when you were branded and you will be with me the entire time, within my view." He paused. "You will have to earn my trust and I won't give it easily so know that I will watch your every move."

"Okay!" She turned, almost slamming into the edge of the bed. "You won't be sorry, Iron. I swear!"

She sidestepped the edge of the bed and almost ran for clothing. She dressed in record time, yanking on her jumpsuit and taking a second to clean her mouth and teeth. She just sat on the floor to put on her boots, not bothering to ask him for socks since hers were dirty. She saw a hand reach down as she finished and grabbed hold of Iron as he tugged her to her feet.

"Don't make me regret this," he warned. "I am already rethinking my impulsive decision."

Staring up into his eyes, she saw worry there. She was shocked he was letting her go so it made sense that he was admitting to not thinking over his invitation. "I'm a good damn mechanic, Iron. I'll work my ass off and I'll be happy to do it."

His hold on her hand tightened. "If you try to run or if you cause me trouble in front of anyone, you will pay for it."

Dawn believed him. "No worries, sexy."

A low growl sounded from his throat. "None of that today."

She managed to hide her amusement as she saluted him with her free hand. "You got it!"

148

Taking a deep breath, Iron looked grim as he gazed down at her. "I mean it, Dawn. Do not make me look bad in front of anyone. I'm a commander and they respect me. I would have to be very harsh with you to set an example. Neither one of us would enjoy that situation if it arose."

He was serious and she realized that, wondering what he'd do to her if she did mess up, but not daring to ask. "I'll be on my best behavior." *At least I'll try*, she thought.

Dawn could barely hide her excitement as Iron activated the doors and moments later she was walking at his side through the *Star*. She had to look at everything and everyone they passed, eager to see anything that was outside of Iron's small quarters. She was led to the *Rally* once again, only this time she wasn't locked up in a cage in the cargo hold. Iron leaned against a wall and then tugged her closer to his body. Their eyes met and held. Eight other cyborg males occupied the cargo area with them, some carrying bags with equipment. Dawn ignored their curious stares directed her way.

"It is a rough trip to the surface. I want you to climb up my body and wrap around me. My friend Flint warned me that it was difficult on his human female with the strong vibrations on the floor. My body will cushion them so it's not as stressful on your more fragile system."

"I've done plenty of rough drops before," Dawn was grateful for his concern. "But thanks. I can handle it."

A red eyebrow arched but he shrugged. "If you change your mind let me know. We're dropping from the *Star* in moments so brace then. You may hold onto me."

She looked up at the mounts high on the wall that Iron reached up to grasp. She was shorter than he was by nearly a foot so she'd have to really stretch up on her tiptoes to reach. She grabbed him around his waist, locking her fingers there, knowing he was just as good to grip as the wall. He was one strong man and she was confident he would not let go of his hold.

There was no warning as the shuttle released. The sudden drop was the first indication the docking clamps had been disengaged. The engines roared to life, vibrating steadily under her feet and in seconds they hit the planet's atmosphere.

Dawn was grateful to be holding onto Iron. She bent her knees a bit and went onto the balls of her feet. It helped with the sharp jarring going up her legs. She was used to rough drops where she worked. The oxygen-making generators were always malfunctioning on the planet's surface, forcing Dawn to repair them. She clung to Iron as the shaking grew worse.

"Climb onto me," Iron ordered her softly.

She shook her head. "It's not so bad. I've been through worse and often. This planet can't be any harsher than Arian Nine was when we first started the conversion."

In minutes the shaking stopped and the floor only vibrated from the engines. They had punched through and would now fly to the surface. That was a smooth ride. Dawn relaxed and her fingers slid a little lower on Iron's body, rubbing the area right over the waist of his pants through his shirt next to his spine.

"What are you doing?"

Dawn glanced up, a grin on her face. "Nothing."

His full mouth curved downward just a hint as he released one of the mounts. His hand curved her waist, gripping her at her hip.

"Dawn…"

"I like touching you," she admitted softly. "No one can see and once we land I have a feeling that we won't get another chance to be this close."

"Behave," he whispered.

"Always," she grinned, whispering back.

Every wicked bone in her body was urging her to do something shocking such as lean up and plant a kiss on his lips with his fellow cyborg pals watching but she refrained. She knew Iron wouldn't see the humor in it and he sure wouldn't kiss her back. With Iron's serious attitude, he'd probably return her right back to his quarters on the *Star*. That dimmed some of her playful spirit.

The shuttle sat down easily, a great skill for a pilot and the engines powered down. The men in the room went instantly in motion, lifting their bags and heading for the docking door. Iron waited until they passed and then he nodded at her.

"Follow them and stay close. You do not speak to anyone. Are my orders clear?"

"Sure. Why can't I talk to people?"

Iron hesitated. "You're my property, Dawn. These aren't cyborgs from Garden. We're civilized but I'm not so certain these cyborgs are. Just follow my orders."

She wasn't sure what that meant but she was going to find out as she followed him down the ramp of the shuttle, getting her first look at the alien planet. Shock tore through her system as she stared at big blue puffy trees, their drooping branches a thick curtain of wispy vegetation. Her gaze lifted to the bright blue sky with light blue clouds, a pretty sight.

"It's beautiful."

Iron led her down the ramp toward thick trees. "It's very blue."

"That's my favorite color."

He glanced down at her. "I'll take note of it."

She grinned. "Okay. You do that."

The encampment they found stunned Dawn as she took it all in with a sweeping gaze. Homes had been built out of bulkheads and spare parts from an obviously large starship. One of the homes had her flinching as she stared at the metal, recognizing just how much of the interior they had salvaged to make homes, knowing the dwelling in question had come from a latrine tank.

"That had to smell pretty bad until they got it clean."

Iron's gaze followed hers. "They are detachable on most of the older ships so it was probably easier for them to remove it to bring it down to the surface."

"That had to have been a shit job, literally."

Dawn could have sworn she saw a smirk on his features before he turned his face away as a noise drew his attention. It also drew Dawn's and she inched away from him to watch as a large group of big gray-skinned women came from the thick woods. The small camp had gone from totally devoid of life to suddenly bursting with it as dozens and dozens of them emerged around them.

Close your mouth, Dawn mentally ordered herself, her eyes going wide with shock at the mostly naked women. Cyborg women were big, muscular, fit, and tall. Most of them wore nothing but half shirts that had seen better days and had made shorts that were tied together to hang low on their hips, exposing a lot of skin and muscled, bulky thighs. Breasts moved freely beneath those thin shirts, revealing that bras weren't considered a cyborg woman's must-have clothing since none of the ones Dawn glanced at wore one.

Behind the women came children. Dawn's body shook slightly as she studied at least two dozen of them. Her heart broke instantly as she saw more than half of them using crutches to limp along. A small boy who was totally naked, probably about three years old, was being carried under his arms by two older girls. His legs were thinner than his body, obviously defective in some manner so he couldn't walk.

"My God." Dawn realized she'd said the words aloud when Iron suddenly spun to softly growl at her.

"Don't look at them." His voice was so low she barely heard his words, her focus jerking away from the children to stare into his furious eyes.

"What is—"

Iron cut her off. "They were left without the technology to fix their children." His tone was soft and gruff. "We can fix them once we get to Garden and some of them before then on the *Star* and the *Vontage*. They are sensitive to their flaws so do not stare or show your disgust."

If he'd slapped her it would have hurt less than what he'd said. "You think I feel disgust?" She hissed the words at him, anger instant. "I feel bad for them and I'm horrified that they have to live this way. My heart is breaking for those children."

He studied Dawn for a long moment. "They just returned from their daily baths at the river. Let's get to work." He jerked his head. "Their shuttle is that way. Move."

Chapter Ten

Dawn was fuming still as she studied the old shuttle in front of them. She wanted to groan as she realized just how old it was. She hadn't seen one of those models since she'd been a kid and her father had taken her to a spaceport to buy parts for an antique shuttle he was restoring for a friend.

"We have to replace the charging cells to restore power, one of the tanks is ruptured, and the entire hull has to be checked. We detected some damage to it so those flaws will have to be patched so it will make it through space."

"Why?" Dawn turned her attention on Iron. "It's old. Hell, I wouldn't trust this rust bucket in space. When your people stole it all those years ago this thing had to be already wrecking-yard standard. It's got to be forty-five years old." She inched away from him to walk to the port thrusters, seeing dents there, and what looked similar to a bird's nest. "I wouldn't trust this thing to lift off and I sure as hell wouldn't want to be aboard her in space." She glanced at him over her shoulder. "I'd be really worried about the integrity of the hull, Iron. This puppy could crush like a tin can because, without tests, which we can't perform here unless you brought a space dock with you to orbit, we don't know what these planet conditions have done to the materials it's made of. It's just not safe."

The cyborgs from the shuttle had followed behind them. One of them, a handsome male with gleaming white hair and dark blue, glittering eyes walked close to Dawn, frowning at her before he turned his attention on Iron.

"She's the mechanic we got from the *Piera* shuttle, correct?"

"Correct, Ice," Iron said softly, looking at Dawn as he spoke. "We're aware of the danger but we aren't transporting them on it. I am going to pilot it back into space myself. We're taking it for salvage."

Dawn faced Iron. "It's too dangerous. If the hull won't hold you'll be killed."

Ice chuckled. "Who gives the orders in your quarters?"

In a heartbeat Iron took a step toward Dawn, going chest to chest with her, anger in his narrowed gaze. "Enough, Dawn. It is my life to risk and I will wear a space suit in case of rapid decompression. I am intelligent and more than aware of the risks. The shuttle has value so we are taking it with us. Once I dock it to the *Moonslip* I will transfer out of it and it will be transported back to Garden."

She feared for his safety. "What if the thing won't make it? It's a dinosaur, Iron. If you have system failure before you break into the atmosphere you'd fall like a rock to the surface. These weren't designed to glide down for easy landings like the modern ones and I doubt it even has an active backup system in place that would enable you to restart the engines if they fail."

"It's my risk to take."

Bullshit, you're mine, she thought but she kept her mouth shut. Her teeth clenched together and she gave him a sharp nod before jerking her attention from him to glare at the shuttle. "I guess I better make damn sure it's fly ready then."

A loud sigh came from behind her as Iron moved away. "Let's get to work. Daylight hours are passing." He started assigning tasks.

Dawn walked over to the thruster and reached up for the rim of it, her hands gripping the bottom and instantly knew she had a problem. Turning her head, she saw that Ice was watching her curiously. She gave him a smile, eyeing his muscular frame.

"Ice?"

An eyebrow arched. "That is my name."

"I'm Dawn. Come here and give me a boost, would you? I don't see a ladder around here so you're it."

Shock made his lips part but to her pleasant surprise he walked toward her. "Why do you want up there?" He stopped inches from her, staring down.

"The thrusters aren't going to clean and inspect themselves. I am going to visually examine the casings and the coils."

His broad chest expanded as he took a deep breath. He gripped her, big hands enclosing over her hips and he lifted. Dawn gripped the rim hard and tensed her body as her feet left the ground. The strong guy easily raised her high enough so she was able to scramble into the large round tube. He shifted his hold on her once she braced her upper weight inside and gave her a gentle push on her lower legs, sending her the rest of the way up. Dawn got to her knees, easily able to kneel inside the generous-sized tube.

"Thanks. Do you have a light on you and perhaps a kit?"

He nodded. "I'll get them."

Dawn turned her attention to the thruster, cringing at the abundant signs of birds taking up residence in the long tube. She knew she'd have to clean it out and then go over every inch of both thrusters on each side of the shuttle. Iron had said they had to replace the charging cells so it wasn't as if they could ignite the thrusters without power while she was inside them.

"Here you go," Ice said from below.

She gave him a smile, accepting the pack he gave her. "Thanks. Please tell Iron I'll be up here."

Ice backed away. Dawn turned her gaze to Iron, whose back was to her while he spoke to two males, one of whom nodded at whatever was being said. She looked away, gripped the repair kit and opened it. She had her work cut out for her. She dug out a power light and flipped it on, getting a better look inside.

"First things first," she muttered as she started to push out dried leaves that had been piled as nests. She used her feet to push it out, inching her way deeper as she cleaned the thruster.

Once she'd cleared it, she started her inspection at the back of the tube. The thruster coils were in better shape than she had hoped, the roof of the thruster casing protecting it from a lot of the elements. She carefully ran a visual inspection for cracks or dents that could create a weak spot but they were in good shape. A female voice drew her from her job.

"Iron?"

Dawn crawled to the end of the thruster tube, curious as to who wanted Iron's attention. In seconds she was peering down to see a tall, mostly naked redheaded cyborg woman standing by the back ramp that led to the interior of the shuttle. The red hair made Dawn tense, wondering if this was the woman from Iron's past.

The cyborg woman was pretty, with flowing red hair just past her bare shoulders. Her skin was a deeper shade of gray, darker than Iron's by far, and the hair was a striking difference in color against her skin. A thick piece of material wrapped around the woman's breasts, holding them in place, and the skirt she wore was low on her hips and almost obscenely short. Dawn gritted her teeth, wondering if the woman wore panties since she hadn't seen a single cyborg woman wear a bra. The skirt rose so high that if the woman bent she'd expose exactly what was under it.

"Fiona," Iron's voice was strong and clear, reaching Dawn's ears easily.

Fiona grinned. "I was on duty but now I am in my off time. I came to see you and I wish to speak to you again about a family unit."

Jealousy and anger burned through Dawn. That was the woman who wanted to take Iron from her. She'd hoped the woman would be ugly but that wasn't the case. While the woman's gray skin was too dark to be really pretty, her features were clearly striking and her muscular body was fit and perfect. Enough skin was showing that Dawn was pretty damn sure the woman didn't have an ounce of excess fat anywhere on her.

"We had this discussion." Iron walked down the ramp and turned his head.

Dawn met his gaze. She resisted the urge to make her presence known to the other woman. Iron looked back at Fiona as his arms crossed over his muscled chest.

"We need to discuss it again." The woman frowned at Iron. "The sex between us was pleasing, we're breeding compatible, and our children would share our unique qualities. It is a perfectly logical choice to join together."

"I am grateful that you thought of me but I have to decline." Iron spun on his heel and began to walk back up the ramp away from the woman.

Fiona grabbed his arm strongly enough to spin him back around. She stepped into Iron, her body pressing against his, revealing that she was just about an inch shorter than he was as their faces nearly touched.

"Take a walk with me and we'll reacquaint our bodies. I have learned much over the years that I believe you will deem a very enjoyable experience."

Dawn saw red and her temper flared to life as Fiona reached down and gripped Iron between his parted thighs, cupping his crotch. It made it worse when Iron didn't jerk away but instead just frowned, totally held himself immobile as he stared at Fiona.

"I have thought of you often," the woman told him. "I will share my thoughts of what I wanted to do with you."

That's it, Dawn thought. She shifted her legs over the outer rim of the thruster tube and turned, gripping the edge hard. She swung her legs, her ass sliding off the edge she'd perched on, and gravity took her. Pain shot up her arms a little when her hands caught her weight so she didn't just

160

drop hard to the ground. She swung twice from the momentum and then released the rim and landed on her feet.

Brushing her sore palms on her jumpsuit, Dawn fixed her attention on the woman who was touching Iron as she stormed quickly toward them. Iron hadn't moved and now the woman was rubbing the seam of his pants, caressing his cock.

"You know it would be good between us and—"

"Get your hands off him!"

Dawn launched herself at the bitch. She grabbed the redhead and clasped the hand on Iron's crotch, pulling the cyborg woman's fingers away and wrenching them brutally back. She yanked her away from Iron. Fiona cried out in pain.

A fist flew at Dawn's face. She jerked her head to the side and knuckles grazed her jaw but the punch didn't land. Dawn used her hold on the fingers locked in her grip to jerk hard on Fiona. Another cry of pain erupted but Dawn was too pissed off to care if she was hurting the bitch who had molested Iron.

A leg shot out that Dawn never saw coming, hitting her in the hip hard enough to knock her off balance. She would have fallen but strong hands grabbed her hips as Iron steadied her.

"Enough," he roared.

Fiona tore her fingers out of Dawn's grasp and threw a punch. Dawn dodged it but it hit Iron in the throat. He made a horrible choking sound, his hands releasing Dawn as he stumbled back. Turning her head, she saw Iron grab his throat as he struggled to breathe and alarm was instant in

Dawn. She hesitated until he sucked in a large breath, obvious that he was recovering. She turned on the cyborg woman with a vengeance.

Dawn tackled Fiona, her body slamming into the woman's firm body, taking them both to the ground. It only took Dawn a second to recuperate as she lifted up by grabbing the woman by her throat with her left hand as she punched her square in the mouth with a right hook. Pain shot up Dawn's arm but she hauled her fist back to nail the bitch again. The second punch never landed as her arm was grabbed by a firm hand and an arm wrapped around her waist. Iron jerked her body off Fiona and backed away from the downed cyborg.

Fiona rolled over, grabbing her face as she sat up. She turned her head, checking her hand for blood but there was none. Her furious glare locked on Dawn. "How dare you attack me?"

"How dare you touch Iron that way," Dawn spat, wiggling in Iron's hold. "Keep your damn hands to yourself." She glared openly at the cyborg. The woman had taken liberties with her man. "He said no to you so get lost."

A frown curved Fiona's lips as she rose to her feet. "You dare speak to me? You dare attack me?"

"I dare." Dawn wasn't one to back down. "Keep your grubby hands off Iron or I'll help you with that little problem you have."

"Dawn!" Iron's tone was harsh. "Enough."

He set Dawn on her feet and then moved between them. He grabbed Fiona, who took a step toward Dawn to go after her.

"Do not, Fiona. She doesn't understand what attacking you means. She is mine so she thinks she is protecting me."

Fiona tore her furious gaze from Dawn to stare at Iron. "She is yours?"

"Yes," Iron confirmed.

Anger darkened the woman's features. "You are having sexual intercourse with a human?"

"Yes. I told you I was in a family unit with one." Iron released Fiona but stayed between Dawn and the furious cyborg female. "She even carries my brand."

"I don't understand."

"You were told that once on Garden you will all be marked with your names on your bodies. Dawn is marked as mine, carrying the same tattoos that I have on my skin."

Shock etched the woman's features as she stared at Iron. "Why would you do that? She's just a human. I thought you were lying to me about being in a unit with one. It sounds so permanent."

"It is."

"That's not acceptable." Green eyes slanted on Dawn. "We will give her to another male. I won't share your attention with a rival female and especially not with the enemy."

"She is not the enemy." Iron paused. "I am contracted in a family unit with her and will never give her to someone else."

Pure rage gripped Fiona's features. "Why would you do that? She's a puny human and you're a valuable rarity."

163

Dawn stepped sideways so she could glare at the other woman. Puny? She wanted to snort. *Okay, maybe I'm short*, she silently admitted, but she knew the other woman was purposely being insulting.

"I wanted the contract." Iron paused. "She is mine and no other male has the right to touch her."

"If that is your reason for rejecting me then I will find other males who are unable to function in that manner. We have two males here that were damaged beyond repair that I could join with so you would be the only male having physical contact with me." Fiona's focus shifted back to Dawn. "She could kill you while you are vulnerable. I would never trust one of those."

"I told you of my decision and it is final. Thank you for the offer but I must refuse." Iron turned and jerked his head toward Dawn. "Go back to work, Dawn. I believe Ice could use you inside the shuttle. He is changing out some damaged wires and your smaller hands would be useful in that task."

Dawn had to resist the urge to argue with him, knowing it would really upset him. The last thing she wanted was to leave him alone with the grabby-handed woman but as she met his intense gaze, she knew she had no choice.

"Sure." Dawn shot a glare at the other woman. "Keep your paws off him."

Fiona took a threatening step toward Dawn. Iron moved fast, stepping between them again. He opened his arms to make sure that Fiona didn't lung at Dawn, protecting her from attack. Moving slowly, Dawn eased by him and walked up the shuttle ramp into the interior. She stepped to the side of the door and froze there, eavesdropping. She didn't feel an ounce of guilt over it either.

"This is unacceptable, Iron." Fury was evident in Fiona's tone. "I have familiarized myself with Garden's breeding laws and family unit contracts since I lead my females. I was given a copy of them when I requested them yesterday. Your genetics and mine are a perfect match for breeding and carrying on our unique traits to future generations. If you refuse to accept my request, I will go before the council we have formed to make them order you to breed with me. Logic will prevail over your fondness for a pathetic human."

"Don't do that, Fiona." Iron's tone was cold. "I don't want you. If you force the issue, you will regret it."

"You are the male I want to breed with and your objections are noted but not a concern of mine."

"I have already been granted family status with the human so you will not get your way."

"Then I will get a list of your breeding pact members and join with them. On the terms of special breeding requirements, code nine-two, I can force you to breed with me. Wouldn't you like access to products we produce? If you refuse a family unit contract, then you would only be a donor with no rights to them."

"I don't want you."

"I do not care what you want," Fiona ground out. "I have been stuck on this planet with only six males to share. They were not males of my specifications but I had to make do with their availability. You are obtainable to me so I will not let this issue go. I am determined to carry on my genes with you as the contributing donor."

"Do what you have to do. I have tasks to complete and my shift time is running down." Iron still sounded furious. "If you want to take this before the council I have no way to stop you but if you do go through my breeding pact to get to me, do not expect the shared sex to be enjoyable. I don't like to be forced to do anything."

Dawn knew the color drained from her face. *Breeding pact? What the hell?* Her mind raced but she didn't know what to think. Could the tall redheaded cyborg somehow force Iron into her bed? Cold fury hit Dawn at the idea of Iron being touched by another woman. No way was she going to allow that to happen.

Easing away from the doorway she walked past the docking doors into the main part of the small shuttle. By current sizes the shuttle was more of a life pod than something to travel in. It would only hold about eight persons in the one room that doubled as a cargo hold and cockpit.

Ice was lying on the floor on his back under one of the piloting stations, his legs bent, and his upper body out of sight. Dawn hesitated and then moved closer.

"I was ordered to help you out."

Silence greeted her statement and then Ice slid out from under the console, inching out enough to stare at her with narrowed eyes. "Get down here then. It is very cramped. They made them too small when this was built."

Work was always good for Dawn while she pondered something. She dropped carefully to her knees and rolled over, getting flat on her back next to the big cyborg. She wiggled under the long panel next to him.

"Good thing we aren't claustrophobic, huh?"

"Speak for yourself," Ice muttered.

Sympathy welled up in her for him as she aligned herself so they were inches apart and she was able to see what he was doing. The smell of burned wire tickled her nose, letting her know he'd been cutting and replacing them. She studied the exposed wires and winced.

"Damn. That's some outdated shit. It's amazing these things didn't catch fire more often, huh?"

Ice grunted.

"You're really talkative, aren't you?"

He turned his head, their faces nearly touching. "Why don't you start with the T wires and I'll work on the N lines?"

She cocked her head, tilting it to glance up at the tools spread out above his head within easy reach. In seconds she had a cutter in hand and was removing some of the frayed wires she found above her.

"What's a breeding pact, Ice?"

The cyborg froze next to her, wire in one hand, cutting tool in the other. "You should ask Iron your questions."

"I'm asking you."

"Ask him." Ice went back to work.

Dawn worked silently, replacing old wire with new for a good ten minutes but then she couldn't stand it anymore. "What are breeding pacts? Can a woman make Iron fuck her because of one?"

The white-haired cyborg refused to look at her. "Ask Iron your questions."

Frustration welled instantly. "If I did that, he'd just blow me off or worse, refuse to answer. Getting shit out of him is like pulling rusty, stripped bolts from an old generator."

A chuckle was her only response. As long seconds turned into a full minute she realized he wasn't going to answer her. She replaced the last wire and then wiggled hard to get out from under the control panel.

"We're not done," Ice called out. "The section next to you also needs replaced. I have been working my way to the starboard."

Dawn climbed to her feet and realized she and Ice were still alone in the shuttle. She bit her lip and then a mean thought struck her. She glanced down at the man's bent legs, the only part of him showing. She wanted answers, damn it, and she wasn't about to risk Iron refusing to answer her since he was the most stubborn man she'd ever met.

One of the repair bags was on top of the control panel as Dawn peered into it. She reached in carefully and removed a metal cutter, a tool about sixteen inches long with pliers-like claws. She gripped it and then stepped between Ice's bent legs, putting the tool right against his thigh. He tensed instantly.

"What are you doing?"

"If you try to wiggle out, that's going to cut you. I asked you a question, damn it. You're claustrophobic, right? Well, now you're stuck and can't get out without a little blood loss. Answer me now. I'm desperate. I hate to do this but I'm not letting the opportunity pass. Tell me all about breeding pacts."

Guilt ate at her for terrorizing the poor guy as she heard his breathing increase. If he moved she'd move the tool, not really ready to cut his leg but he didn't know that. All the cyborgs she'd met so far had a real low opinion of humans so she guessed he might mistake her for being cruel enough to actually hurt him. Just to be safe she turned the sharper edge away, hoping that he wouldn't notice. If he panicked, he could move without meaning to.

"What do you want to know?" His tone was angry and his breathing indicated he wasn't taking the trapped feeling well at all as it increased to a soft pant.

"I just overheard a cyborg woman telling Iron she could hook up with someone in his breeding pact and force him to sleep with her. Is that true?"

"Yes. When I get out of here you're going to pay for this."

"Yeah. I knew it would piss you off. I'm really sorry to have to do this to you but you weren't exactly forthcoming with the explanations when I asked nicely. Tell me how these things work."

"Twelve males sign into a breeding pact. It's law on Garden that we must all breed at least one offspring to further our race. It is highly encouraged to produce more. If a male is damaged—it happens with our

169

kind—someone in his breeding pact must impregnate the female in that family unit." He paused. "Can I get the hell out now?"

"So he just has to donate his sperm?"

Ice's legs started to shake and more guilt slammed Dawn. She had a big guy literally trembling.

"No," Ice panted. "We learned early on that natural breeding works best and the stress involved with artificial insemination causes a high fail rate."

Dawn couldn't make him suffer anymore. She backed away, moving far from him. "Go ahead and get out."

The big cyborg didn't hesitate as he wiggled out from under the console. He was sweating, a sheen of it on his forehead and his upper lip as he sat up. Dawn had a sudden guess as to why he'd been given the name Ice as he gave her the coldest look she'd ever seen while he glared at her. He gripped his bent legs, sitting there, looking furious.

"I'm sorry," Dawn said softly. "This is my life and I have a right to know what the hell is going on. So that woman can hook up with someone in Iron's breeding pact, a male who can't knock her up and she'd be able to force Iron to fuck her? Is that the gist of it?"

Taking deep breaths, Ice continued to glare at her. "Yes."

"What is breeding code nine-two?"

A good minute passed before Ice climbed to his feet, glaring at her still but his shaking had subsided. Meaty fists clenched at his sides and he took a step toward her. Dawn raised the tool the way she would a baseball bat.

170

"Don't even think about it," she warned. "I'm sorry I did that but you shouldn't confess to a weakness and then be a jerk to someone. I did ask you those questions nicely if you'll remember."

He froze in his tracks but still looked ready to lunge at her to get even. His icy gaze went to the weapon in her hand and then returned to lock hers. "It means that there's something inherently special or unique about someone that requires them to breed with another similar to them."

"Is red hair considered unique to your kind?"

His head jerked in a nod. "Red hair and white." He reached up to touch his hair, a finger brushing it before his hand dropped. "I know that code due to its use on me five times so far by females who requested my DNA. I denied their requests. They took me before the council and I was ordered to donate."

"Did you get angry about it? They really order you to have sex with women? Doesn't that really bother you?"

He nodded again. "Regardless of your human ignorance, we aren't unfeeling. If you think I enjoy being a donor to children I have no right to see or get to know, you are incorrect, but it is the law. We all must make sacrifices to survive." He clenched his teeth. "Humans left us no other choice in the matter but to go to drastic measures to ensure our survival." Pain flashed in his eyes.

Dawn dropped the weapon and took a step toward him, sympathy welling up inside her for this man. She wanted to wince as she lifted her chin. "Go ahead. Do you want to take a shot at me for what I did? I deserve it. Could you try not to break something though? I didn't really hurt you and I had no intention of drawing blood."

Shock gripped his features. "I don't plan on hitting you. I only wanted to take your weapon from you before one of us got harmed."

Her body relaxed. "Oh."

Disgust twisted his features. "That's a human response. I'm far above your standards of behavior." He took a deep breath. "Do not ever do that again. We have work to do and I have regained control of my systems. I was locked up and tortured." His voice deepened. "It is an unreasonable fear but it is there all the same."

"I am sorry."

He just glared at her for a long moment. "Get back to work, and if you ever do that again, you will wish that striking you like a human would be my response."

He turned his back on her and lowered his big body to the floor again. He hesitated but then slowly inched back under the control panel. Dawn walked forward. She had a lot of thinking to do and working always helped her figure things out.

Chapter Eleven

"What did you do?"

Dawn started at Iron's words as he came up behind her where she sat eating lunch on the edge of the small hillside the shuttle sat on. She turned her head to give him the most innocent look she could muster. "I haven't done anything."

Had Ice told on her? Probably. She noticed Iron's tight, angry expression. Iron looked downright irritated as he hovered over her. While she'd worked side by side with Ice after what she'd done to him, he'd relaxed and even made a few jokes about the old shuttle they were working on. She'd hoped he'd give her a break and not tell Iron but she'd been wrong.

"The stabilizer grid is totally re-wired and you took the gravity control offline from what I have determined."

She pushed air from her lungs, relief slamming her. She owed Ice and made a mental note to thank him for not ratting her out. "You said you can remote link with your..." She tapped her head. "Implants. All the relays for the manual control were fried beyond repair. Ice said you don't have replacements for them and it would take days to try to create something that can replace them since everything is so outdated. You don't have anything available that will work. You said you're just going to fly it into space to dock to the *Moonslip* so it will work fine for you short term. If you had to fly it for an extended distance or time I wouldn't have gone that way."

"I see." Iron hesitated and then sat down next to her. He straddled the log she was using for a chair. "I am glad that my orders were followed and they brought you food."

"It's weird but good." She offered her plate to him. "Try the green plant thing. It's kind of like a banana in the shape and the way it peels but it tastes similar to mushy maple syrup. It's really sweet but not too over the top that it's sickening."

He didn't hesitate to grab up the fruit as a smile played on his lips. "I am proud of you, Dawn. You have behaved extremely well."

Heat flushed her cheeks as she looked away and hoped he didn't notice it. "Thanks." If only he knew.

"We will return to the *Star* soon."

She didn't want to be reminded of being back in his small room. She enjoyed the fresh air work too much. She dreaded going back to the ship and back to her confinement.

"Iron?"

A black-haired cyborg paused near them. "We're ready to run the engine tests and we need you there. What is your range of transmissions and receiving?"

"Approximately thirty feet." His attention returned to Dawn. "Stay here in case there are problems. I want you at a safe distance. The shuttle hasn't been used in at least ten years."

"You're going to be on the outside, right?"

174

He nodded as he popped the fruit he'd peeled into his mouth. Standing up slowly, he stepped over the log to walk away. Dawn turned to watch him approach the shuttle, worried that something would go wrong. She noticed the cyborgs moved away from the shuttle a safe distance while Iron moved to the front of it, close to the nose and away from the thrusters at the back.

Dawn held her breath as Iron closed his eyes, an expression of concentration on his face. She assumed he linked mentally with the onboard computer. The engine came online—a loud, rough sound. She inhaled slowly as the sound increased and smoothed out a little as it warmed up. The back thrusters burned, shooting fire for seconds, making Dawn wince at the old way the shuttles used to fire literally. The thrusters turned, making a slight squeaking sound that could be heard over the engines and then the shuttle lifted a few feet from the ground.

It amazed her that Iron could stand on the ground and control the ship but it was obvious that he did. He opened his eyes, his hands fisted at his sides, and intently watched the hovering ship. He eased it back down and powered down the thrusters. He kept the engines on but he did open the back hatch so two cyborgs could go inside to check the systems visually.

Turning away from him she peered at the sight below her where she could see the small cyborg camp. A line of trees separated the living area from the river. She had a good view of both from a side angle. Movement caught her attention by the river as someone stepped out of the trees toward the water.

There was an outcropping of rocks leading out into the river as if someone had painstakingly made a dock of sorts that jutted about fifteen feet from the river's edge. A small child, perhaps six years old, walked out onto it. He wore braces on his legs, easily seen even from a hundred yards away since they were thick and he walked with a heavy limp. He held what Dawn assumed was a fishing pole as he edged to the end of the rocks. A frown twisted her lips as he stumbled a little on the rocks but then caught his balance. It looked dangerous for a kid on braces to try to navigate the wide rocky path.

She blew out a breath when the kid reached the end to a flatter smooth-surfaced rock and threw out his line. He looked as if he knew what he was doing but her gaze scanned the area around him, trying to locate an adult who should be watching him. There was no one, unless they were out of her sight in the tree line. It was possible with those thick, dangling branches that worked the way curtains would. She turned her head and watched as Iron walked around the shuttle to the back and up the ramp to disappear inside. Dawn turned her head and automatically her attention went to the cyborg boy.

Memories of when she was a child with her family instantly came to mind. Every summer her family had gone camping until she and her siblings had hit their teens. Her father had taught her how to fish and she found it endearing that cyborg children were a hell of a lot similar to human ones. A smile curved her lips as the little boy tossed his line again, telling her that he was a fly fisherman.

He was sending out his line again minutes later when disaster struck. He stepped back, probably not realizing that he was too close to the edge of the rock he stood on, and she saw him lose his balance, tilt backward, his arms waving wildly, almost as if he were trying to use them for wings to take flight. He hit the water without even making a splash. Dawn's mouth opened up in horror but she held still waiting for him to swim up to the surface. In seconds, when he didn't, she realized he was in trouble.

She turned her head but Iron and the cyborgs working with him were inside the shuttle. She looked down the steep embankment in front of her and then was moving. Iron wouldn't hear her yell over the engines and she didn't have time to run his way to get help. The boy wasn't coming up and she knew seconds counted and she inwardly winced as she went over the edge.

Her boots struck dirt and her butt hit hard on the harsh hillside as she started to slide on her ass. The steep decline made her pray she didn't lose control as she tried to use her boots to steer as gravity made her pick up speed. Dirt and dried leaves slowed her a little but then she hit the bottom hard. Pain shot through one ankle as she forced herself to her feet, not even bothering to brush off her ass or back as she started to run.

She couldn't see the water but she could see the dock as she sprinted around bushes on her rush to the river. Pure panic hit her as she reached the dock, out of breath. She didn't see a little dark head on the surface. The water was almost still, no obvious current to drag his body away but it wouldn't take much. She hit the rocks leading out on the dock, panting hard, but she kept moving until she reached the end.

Her gaze frantically scanned the surface but she didn't see him. His pole was crushed under her boot where he'd dropped it. She turned her head but saw no help, no one by the trees, and as she looked up where she'd been sitting, no Iron standing there to see where the hell she'd gone. She was alone. As Dawn jerked her focus back on the water, she saw something there that just bobbed to the surface for a second about eight feet to her right. It had looked like little fingers.

Dawn dove in headfirst, not bothering to remove her boots. The kid had been in the water for probably close to two minutes. The water was shockingly cold as her body hit and she lost all sense of up or down. It was just cold and wet. She had aimed at her target so she blindly reached for him, her hands seeking as she widened her arms up and down and to the sides. Her wrist brushed something and she reached back thinking it was hair. It had to be from the soft brush her fingers ran through. She carefully followed it down and hit something rounded—the size of the boy's head. She used both hands to grab as she found a shoulder and his ribs, clutching him while she tried to find the bottom of the river with her feet. She couldn't find solid ground but she couldn't be sure that was the right direction of where the bottom should be.

She clung to him but then relaxed the rest of her body, feeling herself float in one direction. She knew that had to be up so she dragged his body against hers, noticing that he was still, not fighting, and not clutching her. One arm wrapped around his body while she used her legs and free hand to swim. In seconds she broke the surface and she gasped in much needed air.

She shook her head hard to clear wet hair from her eyes, desperately seeking the direction of land. She saw it behind her so she maneuvered in that direction, swimming hard and frantically for it. When her boot kicked ground she almost sobbed with relief, fighting the boy's limp weight and trying to negotiate between water and finding balance to lurch toward the embankment. The kid was little but he was heavy. She got them both to the edge and then she carefully laid him down so he was face up and mostly out of the water.

He was gray, even for a cyborg. He wasn't breathing and his eyes were closed. Panic and horror hit Dawn knowing he'd drowned. She was gasping for breath, freezing cold, soaking wet, and desperately trying to remember first aid. She grabbed the boy, tipping his head back, and crawled to his side. Bending low, she covered his parted mouth and blew air into him while she gently pinched his nose closed. She turned her eyes, watching his chest lift. It was working but would she be able to revive him? She wasn't sure.

She started chest compressions, terrified she'd break his fragile ribs, being careful to not apply too much pressure to his chest. She gave him another breath and as she lifted up to start compressions, he started to choke. Relief nearly floored Dawn as she turned him on his side, hot tears filling her eyes as he gasped in air, coughing, sputtering, and struggling to breathe but he was alive.

Rolling him more onto his stomach than not, Dawn supported his small body with one arm around his chest and rubbed him with her other hand on his back. "It's all right," she tried to soothe him. "Just stay with me. You're out of the water."

He finally stopped choking but his breaths were harsh and strained. Dawn turned her head, looking for help again but no one was in view near the trees or up on the hill she'd come from. Anger flashed through her, caused by her fear for the little boy and frustration that no one was there to help. Didn't Iron notice she was gone? Where the hell were this kid's parents? She pushed those questions screaming through her mind back and instead realized she would have to find help since it wasn't coming to her.

The little boy turned his head, staring at her with pretty light green eyes set behind long, black eyelashes. His color was less dark gray and more of a dull nickel shade. She hoped that meant he was doing better, not familiar with his normal shade of gray. Terror filled his eyes as he stared up at Dawn.

"Hey, it's okay," she said softly. "You're safe now. I got you out of the water and now I'm going to try to carry you back to camp to see if we can find a doctor."

"You're full human," his little voice shook, terror still widening his eyes.

What had they taught this little boy about humans? It made her want to cringe. "Look," Dawn said softly. "I'm not going to hurt you. Do you remember falling into the water?"

He gave a shaky nod.

"I was helping work on a shuttle with a few cyborgs like you and I saw you fall in. I pulled you out. I wanted to save you, okay? Not hurt you."

He blinked at her and then bit his lower lip. "You won't kill me?" He swallowed hard, his little throat tightening for a second. "Humans kill cyborgs."

"I don't." Dawn forced a smile. "What is your name?"

"Davton."

He had an odd name but Dawn didn't say that aloud. "If I stand up and bend down, do you think you could wrap your arms around my neck? I am going to lift you up and carry you back to your camp."

He nodded bravely as another coughing fit seized him while Dawn got to her feet, urging her to hurry it along to get help for the boy. Her toes rubbed in a bad way in her wet boots that were super heavy as she shifted her stance. She bent forward to allow the kid to grip her and she slid her hands under his small body. She noticed then that one of his braces was broken.

She lifted him in her arms and wanted to groan. He weighed more than any of her nephews and nieces did at that age even though he was deceptively thin. She wondered if it were the braces that gave him at least an extra thirty pounds of weight but it didn't matter. She had to carry him to get help. She sure wasn't about to leave him alone while he was afraid or in danger of choking to death from his fits of coughing.

"I'm Dawn," she told him softly, planting one wet, heavy boot in front of another. She was shaking from the cold and her clothes were sticking to her, rubbing her skin raw. "Do you always go fishing by yourself?"

"No. My mother usually takes me but she had to make some calls from one of those big ships that are here to rescue us. My brace got caught on something and I couldn't swim." His arms tightened around her neck. "Do you know where I live?"

"I know where the camp is. It's just past those trees." She gripped him a little higher, the muscles in her arms protesting at his heavy weight but kept moving. "Do me a favor, Davton. Never go fishing or by the river by

181

yourself again, all right? Even adults should always go with a buddy. Do you know what the buddy system is?"

"No."

"It's where you go do things with a friend so if one of you gets hurt or into trouble the other one can go for help."

"I am a cyborg. We have to be self sufficient to survive and we can never trust someone else to watch our back. My mother taught me that it is better to be solitary."

Dawn stopped walking, her attention going from the ground in front of her to the sweet little boy face inches from her shoulder. Horrified shock tore through her at his matter-of-fact words. "We all need someone sometimes, kiddo. Human, cyborg, puppy dog, or birdie in the sky, we all have that in common."

"Do you need anyone?"

Iron's image came to mind instantly. "Yeah. I do and I'm afraid sometimes to trust him but you just have to learn to have faith in someone."

Davton studied her until a shiver shook him. "I will try to find a buddy to share a system with."

A smile played at her lips as she started to walk again. Her boots made a loud noise with each step, water squishing out of them but she started to warm from the movement. She walked through the fifty feet of tree line and the thick drapes of branches into the open cyborg camp. She paused there with the boy in her arms, wondering how long it would take before

182

someone saw her. She estimated she had maybe twenty seconds. It was closer to five.

The camp went dead silent as heads turned to stare openly at Dawn. "Do you have a doctor? He fell in the river and stopped breathing."

One woman, a large dark-haired cyborg, dropped a pot of water by the fire and ran toward Dawn. She almost tore Davton out of Dawn's arms, spinning to rush the boy away into one of the constructed homes. Dawn stood there and let her arms drop. Another woman marched toward Dawn, anger etched on her features. She lunged, grabbing Dawn by the front of her jumpsuit, fisting it in her hand.

"What did you do to Davton?"

"I didn't do anything to him. I saw him fall in the river and dove in after him."

Dawn resisted the urge to tear herself out of the other woman's hold. She kept her voice loud and steady though, judging by some of the looks on the cyborg women's faces, she wasn't welcome in the least. A shiver of fear jolted down her spine as at least ten of them surrounded her, all the women looking furious as they glared. She knew she was in a world of shit.

"He fell into the water while fishing." She stared directly into the woman's furious gaze who gripped her. "I saw it from the hill where I was taking a lunch break and rushed down to pull him out. I came with Iron to help work on the shuttle."

The woman frowned and her hold on Dawn's wet jumpsuit loosened. "He wasn't breathing?"

Shaking her head, Dawn relaxed slightly. "I was able to revive him but he needs a doctor. He's been coughing up water so it got into his lungs."

The woman turned. "Contact the *Vontage* and tell them we either need their medic sent to us or Davton picked up to be taken to their ship now, Viper."

A dark-haired cyborg shot Dawn a glare before she rushed off. Dawn swallowed the lump that formed in her throat. "I need to get back to Iron. I don't think he realizes I'm gone. They were inside the shuttle testing the systems when I saw the boy fall in. I didn't have time to get help since I knew seconds counted."

"What is your name?"

"Dawn."

"I'm Plono." The woman released Dawn and took a step back. "You will remain here until I speak to the boy to make sure you are telling the truth and then I will escort you back to the repair crew on the hill working on the *Yas*."

"*Yas*?"

"The shuttle. The paint faded but that is her name."

"Okay." Dawn knew it wasn't up for debate. She shivered, chills racking her body from being cold and wet. "Can I sit by the fire? I'm freezing."

The woman hesitated and then nodded, stepping out of the way. "Stay by the fire and make no sudden movements." Plono glanced at the women around them. "Watch her." Without another word the woman spun away, heading for where Davton had been taken.

184

Dawn moved slowly to the fire and sat down on one of the stones around the pit that had been laid out. She tore off her boots and placed them near enough to the fire to start drying without being in danger of getting too hot or burning. She glanced around her at the unusually quiet camp, seeing that all eyes were on her.

The fire wasn't doing much to warm her but it was better than nothing. She was soaked all the way to her skin. In minutes Plono returned, looking less angry as she approached Dawn.

"We are grateful you saved the boy." The woman cyborg looked anything but happy to be indebted to a human. "If you will follow me, I'll find you some dry clothing before you grow ill and then I'll return you to your work duty."

The idea of being in something dry and getting warm was welcome to Dawn as she stood up. "Thanks. I'd appreciate it."

"Follow me."

Dawn left her boots behind to dry a little more as she walked barefoot through the camp toward one of the larger homes that near the back. Plono opened the door and waved Dawn inside. Without hesitation Dawn walked into the dim room. It took her seconds of blinking to adjust from daylight to the interior.

The room was probably eighteen by twelve feet with a ten-foot-high ceiling. Metal made the walls shine a little. A bed dominated a corner of the room, a big four poster made out of blue tree branches. Shock tore through Dawn as she stared at the bed. It wasn't so much the bed that held her attention, but what was on it.

"That's Coal. Ignore him," Plono ordered Dawn, moving to a stack of crates that was used as an open dresser with clothing stacked inside.

Dawn's mouth was hanging open and she couldn't look away to save her life. A big, bald cyborg male was tied spread eagle to the headboard and footboards. Only a sheet covered his lap but the rest of his thickly muscled body was exposed. He lifted his head to glare at Dawn. She met his dark brown stare.

"I said ignore him," Plono said louder.

Dawn tore her stunned gaze from the man. "Why is he tied down?"

Plono grabbed some clothing and turned. The cyborg woman glanced at the bed and then walked to Dawn. "He is being punished. Put these on."

"But…" She glanced around the room. "There's nowhere that's private. There are no walls or anything." Her focus went back to the tied male.

"Your point is?"

"He'll see me if I change in here." Dawn stared up at her hostess.

"He has seen many females without their clothing on. He's our breeder. Change your clothing quickly or don't. I won't—"

The door opened and Viper stepped in. "The *Vontage* is sending a shuttle but they wish to speak to you now."

Plono moved quickly toward the door. "Stay here, human. I will return shortly and then escort you back to your work crew. If you leave my home it will be considered a threat against my females."

In stunned silence Dawn stood there staring at the male tied to the bed after they were left alone. He frowned at her and then tugged his arms but they were tied at the wrist. When he spoke, his voice was unnaturally deep and a little rough as if he didn't use it much.

"Do you plan on just staring at me?"

"I'm sorry." She flushed, her cheeks heating up. "Why are you tied down? What are you being punished for?"

"I escaped and they had to track me down." A cold smile angled his full lips upward. "It took them two months to find me this time so now they are keeping me tied up around the clock and they send fifteen women with me when they allow me to go to the river to bathe."

"You're a cyborg. Why would you try to escape from your own people?"

He jerked on the rope again, the wood creaking but not giving way. "You're a slave as much as I am. Did your ship crash here?"

"No. I'm with some cyborgs who came here to rescue the survivors of the *Moonslip*. That would be you. No one told you?"

A deep growl tore from his lips as he twisted again in his ropes, this time using his legs as well. The sheet moved, sliding dangerously low on his hips. Dawn averted her gaze, not wanting to embarrass him, suspecting that he wore nothing under that sheet.

"No one told me. They don't talk to me much unless it's to give orders."

"But you're a cyborg."

He frowned. "Change your clothing or they will return you to work that way."

"I'm not stripping naked in front of you."

A black eyebrow arched. "Modesty?"

"I guess so."

He twisted again, pulling on the rope but unable to break free. "I will close my eyes. You shouldn't suffer needlessly for having a rare female trait."

A rare female trait? Was he for real? Dawn watched him lower his head and close his eyes. She hesitated and then quickly stripped out of her wet jumpsuit, the material sticking to her. She shivered as she put on a threadbare shirt and a pair of large cut-off pants with a tie waist. The clothes were old and nearly falling apart at the seams but they were dry against her skin and really large.

"I'm done. Thanks."

He opened his eyes, lifted his head, and gave her a nod. "Will you do me a courtesy?"

"What do you want?"

"Will you tell your owners about me? Tell them I wish to have a discussion about earning my freedom. Are you owned by males or females?"

"Male. Singular." Dawn glanced around the room and then moved to the table by the door. She grabbed the small item and moved toward the bed. "I'll tell him but instead of asking for that, why not ask for this?" She held up the steak knife. "I'd want to be cut loose."

Shock stunned his features. "Your male will punish you for freeing me."

Dawn put her knee on the bed, going for the wrist closest to her. She shrugged. "What is Iron going to do? Yell at me?" She snorted. "Not talk to me for a day? I'll survive."

The knife wasn't very sharp so she really had to saw through the thick rope but she managed it. He still looked amazed as he snatched the knife from her fingers, turning to hack through the rope gripping his other wrist.

"Tell your male I forced you to free me to avoid harsh punishment," he said softly. "I owe you a favor."

"You don't owe me a thing," Dawn said backing away from the bed. "But you might want to wait to free yourself until I'm out of here or that woman is going to be back here real soon to see you're loose."

He hesitated, turning his head to stare at her. A slow smile spread across his features. "We could both escape. I will take you with me into the mountains. They will eventually capture us again but we'll both be free until then."

Dawn backed up. "No thanks. I don't want to go anywhere but back to Iron."

The cyborg stared at her with a confused expression. Dawn sighed.

"I love him. I'm working on making him love me back. He might threaten to put me over his knee or tie me to his bed but he won't hurt me."

Coal cut his legs loose and then sliced through the rope that was tied to the frame, taking all of it with him as he climbed off the bed. Dawn

189

gasped and spun around to present him with her back as he stalked totally naked to the crates of clothing, obviously comfortable in his bare skin.

In less than a minute the man had a pair of pants on and was grabbing things around the room. Dawn watched him silently as he used a sheet to gather supplies. He was smart to grab things while he could if he planned on going into the mountains. She noticed he kept hold of the rope.

"You're taking hacked rope?"

He paused, meeting her gaze. "Tell them I pulled free. If there is no evidence left behind they won't know you cut me loose." He stared down at her. "Are you sure you do not wish to flee with me? I won't harm you."

"I'm sure but thanks for the offer. Good luck with running but instead of doing that, why don't you go talk to the cyborgs who came to rescue you?"

"Their females in charge will just hand me over to my females so there is no point."

"There aren't any females in charge on the *Star*. That's the ship I came on. I was told the men outnumber the females on the cyborg home planet."

His features showed his shock. "Are you sure?"

She nodded. "Go to the hill where the *Yas* is. Iron, the guy who owns me, is up there with a crew of his men fixing the shuttle. That's where I came from today."

He moved to the corner, studying it, and then was shifting the metal wall to open it up a few feet to reveal the outside and trees. He glanced back at Dawn, staring at her for a long moment before he slipped out of the room.

Dawn sighed and walked to the front door. She hesitated, wondering how much shit she would get into if she just waited on the outside. It might give Coal a little more running time if no one came in to see he was gone. She lifted her chin, pushed on the door and stepped outside.

She saw Iron storming toward her, looking enraged. Ice was on his heels.

"Dawn, I warned you not to run," Iron snarled.

"I didn't. There was a boy who—"

Iron reached her, his hands wrapping around her as he jerked her against his body. He held her there, lowering his head to hers and a strong arm wrapped around her.

"I was worried." He said softly.

"A boy fell in the water and I pulled him out. I'd never run from you."

Iron sighed. "I will punish you if you're lying. They will tell me the truth."

So much for trust. Dawn sighed as Iron released her. She saw Plono heading their way from another house. *It sucks,* Dawn thought, *that he needs verification instead of just believing me.*

Chapter Twelve

"She freed my male," Plono was furious as she glared at Dawn.

A deep frown was fixed on Iron's features. "What male?"

The fuming cyborg woman hesitated as a look of dread flashed on her face before it disappeared. "I have a slave."

Iron jerked his head toward Ice. "Alert our men that there is a hostile human free. He might go for the *Rally*."

"He's not human," Dawn said softly. When Iron's head jerked her way, she met his stunned gaze. "He's a cyborg."

"What in the hell is going on?" Ice stepped forward, glaring at Plono. "You enslaved one of our men? Why?"

"He was the only breeding male. The others were sterile. We tried but only Coal was able to produce for us. He refused to service our women so we had to take measures to force him to comply. After he started running from us and we were forced to track him countless times, we changed his status from free to slave." Plono glared back at Ice. "All of our children are from him. Would you prefer that we did not breed?"

"Fuck," Ice cursed. "You forced him?" Rage curved his hands into fists and his body tensed. "You enslaved him? Turned him into a breeding machine for any of your females who wished to have children? Is that what you're saying?"

"It was the only option he left us with." Her full focus turned on Dawn. "She freed him. I know he couldn't have broken loose himself. I tied him down personally. I demand she be punished."

The woman who had taken Davton from Dawn earlier stepped forward. "She saved the life of my son, Plono. She deserves mercy for that."

Irritation flashed on the cyborg woman's face. "Fine. I will only give her ten lashes instead of twenty for her helping my male escape." She shot a dirty look at Iron. "You will help find him since your slave freed him. That is fair."

Iron gripped Dawn's arm. "If you touch my human I'll take a whip to you and give you twenty lashes. No one touches her but me." He jerked his head at Ice. "Let's go. We're going back to the *Star* and have a conversation with Steel and Flint over this."

"What about my male?" Plono was still angry. "We are leaving the planet soon and without your assistance we won't be able to find him. He is very cunning at hiding from us."

"We'll find him," Ice hissed. "And we'll make damn sure he's off this planet and out of your control."

"He's mine," Plono took a threatening step toward Ice.

"Enough," Iron ground out. "We will find the male and then address his status."

Ice shot a disbelieving look at Iron. Iron met his gaze and nodded. "We need to get back to the *Star* now to have that meeting."

Relief flooded Dawn as she walked away with Iron and Ice, leaving the small camp behind them. As soon as they were out of earshot, Ice spoke.

"We're going to find this male and make sure those females don't get their hands on him again."

"Agreed," Iron sighed. "I didn't want to fight with them. What they did was wrong but who knows what the council will decide. He was the only viable male but most of the council will have issues with his becoming a slave. Our main objective now is making Steel and Flint aware and to find this male."

"His name is Coal," Dawn offered. "He's about six-foot-four, really buff, with dark brown eyes and he's bald."

Iron stopped walking, studying Dawn. "Did you free him or did he break loose?"

"I cut the ropes." She lifted her chin, daring Iron to get mad at her over it. "They had him tied down naked to a bed and I was ordered to ignore him like he didn't exist. It pissed me off." She hesitated. "I told him to head for the shuttle we were working on and that I thought you'd help him. He thinks women rule all the men and that your women will just hand him back over to those bitches back there. I told him men outnumber women."

Ice sighed. "Perhaps he will come to us so we don't have to look for him."

"Perhaps." Iron let his hand trail down Dawn's arm to her hand, which he grasped. "I worried that you'd run from me. I am proud that you saved the small child's life."

"I just hope your doctors can fix his legs. It never would have happened if he wasn't in those heavy leg braces."

Iron studied her eyes. "You care about him."

194

"He's a little kid. Everyone should care about them."

"He's a cyborg."

Dawn snorted. "So?"

Iron looked away from her. "Let's go."

Her gaze wandered the area around them, hoping to spot Coal but when they reached the old shuttle no one but Iron's men were there. He gave them an update and then led Dawn back to where the *Rally* had landed. Ice had stayed behind to keep an eye out for Coal in case he showed up looking for help.

Depression flooded Dawn as they left the planet's surface. She realized Iron was watching her as she sat on the cargo hold floor near him. Turning her head, she met his narrowed gaze.

"Are you well, Dawn?"

"I'm bummed."

That drew a frown from him.

"You're going to lock me back up in our quarters."

His features softened with understanding. "My meeting won't run long and then I'll be back to *my* quarters."

She didn't miss how she had said "our quarters" and he'd said "my" with a definite emphasis on it. It might be habit for him to talk in the singular but she doubted it. She guessed it was a gentle reminder that he owned everything and that included her. Pain sliced through her chest.

After Iron left her locked inside their quarters, Dawn stripped out of the borrowed clothing, going into the cleansing unit immediately to wash the river smell from her hair and body. She leaned against the wall as foam hit her, her thoughts all centered on Iron and his stubborn pride. Would it kill him to relax and not try to put walls between them? First it was his issue of not sleeping with her and now he was trying to keep her at arm's length with petty wording.

The foam made her body tingle as it melted to liquid. She climbed out, tersely drying off with one of Iron's thick towels. She had to do something or she was going to be miserable. That wasn't acceptable. Dawn shook her head. No way was she going to live with a man who made her unhappy. She dropped the towel, walked to the bed and stretched out naked on it.

Fiona was bothering her as well. Would the woman be able to force Iron into her bed? If Dawn could go back in time she would have hit her harder when she'd punched her in the face. The cyborg seemed damn determined to make little redheaded babies with Iron. Dawn clenched her teeth and raw jealousy poured through her at the thought of him touching another woman, willing or not. He was hers, carried her name on his body, and they were married.

She got up and put on one of Iron's shirts. It fell almost to her knees, so baggy she almost laughed. Her mood wouldn't allow it though as she paced. If they went back to the cyborg planet and the council sided with Fiona, Iron would be forced to breed with that green-eyed bitch. He'd probably be tied to a bed and forced to suffer her touch the way poor Coal had been, forced to endure whatever the women who wanted him did to him while trying to get pregnant by using him as a stud.

Dawn started to worry as minutes turned into hours. Finally, the door opened to admit Iron. One glance at his features told her he was furious as he stepped inside and let the doors close behind him. Their gazes met and held. She walked right up to him to put her hands on his chest.

"What's wrong?"

A muscle along his jaw jumped as he unclenched his teeth. "We recovered Coal. He walked right up to Ice and introduced himself so we brought him aboard the *Star*. We listened to his story and then contacted the cyborg council to inform them of his mistreatment by the females from the *Moonslip*. They in turn contacted the surface, relaying the signals through the *Vontage*. Fiona and Plono made a strong case for their actions to the council since he was the only male with naturally viable sperm they could use. They aren't going to hold those females accountable for making a slave of one of our males."

"So they just get away with it?" A horrible thought struck her. "Are they ordering you to return him to them? You won't do it, will you?"

"They aren't ordering that. They were horrified at hearing of his treatment and he's been assigned to the *Star* so no women are near him unless he wants them to be. The women will be transferred to Garden so they will have access to many males yet Plono still argued to try to keep him. She really angered me and the other males. Coal is safe now on the *Star* where he will remain. As of this moment he is in his private quarters down the hall."

"Thank God." She sighed, relaxing for a moment. "That poor man."

Cocking his head, Iron frowned at her. "You care for him?" Something flickered in his eyes.

Dawn arched an eyebrow. "Are you jealous? Don't be." Her fingers explored his uniform shirt as her morose thoughts returned. "I just feel bad for him. They forced him to have sex with whatever woman wanted to get knocked up, tied him to a bed, and kept him as a slave. That would be a horrible life for anyone but I imagine it is worse for a big, strapping male. It had to play hell with his ego."

"You are spending a lot of time considering how it affected him." Anger simmered in Iron's beautiful blue eyes. "Are you sure you aren't drawn to him?"

"You are jealous." Dawn couldn't help but grin, a warm feeling spreading through her chest. "You do care about me."

Iron's entire body tensed. "You find this amusing that I don't enjoy the concept of you being drawn to another male?" He wrapped his arms around her waist. "You are mine, Dawn. Never forget that. I won't share your body or space in your thoughts with another man."

"The only thing I'm thinking about is you." She started unbuttoning his shirt. "And getting you naked." She glanced up at him. "And then having hot, sweaty sex together."

"Are you sure you aren't drawn to him?" Iron searched her eyes with his intense gaze.

"Sexy, you're the only man I'm drawn to. I swear." She pushed open his shirt, lowering her focus to his broad chest. "You take my breath away. You're a guy, but damn are you beautiful. I just want to run my hands over every inch of your skin and lick you in the worst way."

He took a sharp breath and blood swelled into his cock, bringing it to life as it hardened against her where he pressed into her stomach. She loved that he reacted so strongly to her. She rid him of his shirt and started on the front of his pants as she eased back. He released her as she removed his belt and dropped it to the floor. His pants went down to his ankles and she shoved his briefs down too. She went to her knees before him and he lifted his feet to help her as she removed his boots and socks.

When she'd freed him of everything she straightened on her knees, inspecting a very aroused cock inches in front of her face. "I think I should start here."

"Dawn," he said softly. "Don't tease."

Lifting her gaze to peer up at him, she smiled, licked her lips, and then breathed on the tip of his cock, which pointed at her. "Sexy, it's only teasing if I don't aim to please and I do." Her hand wrapped around the base of his shaft as she opened her mouth.

She thought about teasing him but then just took him fully inside her mouth, wrapping around a good four inches of him. Her tongue rubbed the underside of his cock as she suckled on him, her hand slowly pumping hard flesh. A soft groan was Iron's response. His fingers slid into her hair, cupping the side of her head to massage her scalp. Her other hand slid up his inner thigh to his sac where she lightly raked her fingernails on the underside before cupping to gently massage.

Tilting her head, she took more of him until he neared the back of her throat, slowly sucking as she pulled back, almost releasing him but not letting go. She suddenly pushed forward, taking him again, turning her head straight and then set a steady pace, repeating the maneuver.

"What you do to me," Iron softly groaned.

She knew what that was as his cock hardened even more, taking on the consistency of his name. His sweet flavor teased her taste buds as pre-cum eased out onto her tongue. She moaned around him and his other hand slid into her hair, his fingers lightly gripping the sides of her head. His balls drew up in her palm, the skin tightening. She knew he was going to come when he started to move his hips in counter sync to her mouth. She slowed the pace and then eased him out of her mouth fully. Dawn opened her eyes and leaned back a little to stare up at him.

Iron's face was flushed with passion and his beautiful gaze locked on hers. "Why did you stop?"

She released his sac and stood up. "I want you flat on the bed."

He hesitated but then moved. She loved watching him walk. He was so hard his cock bounced with every step. She stared at his beautiful ass, loving the round fullness of it and the muscles that flexed as he walked. He stretched out on his back on the bed, his gaze locked on her as she slowly approached him.

"Climb on me," he ordered softly. "Ride me."

She was tempted but then she smiled. "Ever done sixty-nine?"

"No." He frowned. "What is that?"

Dawn grinned as she put her knee on the bed. "You're bottom." She glanced at his impressive manhood. "I'm afraid you'd choke me so you're definitely bottom. Scoot down some so your legs are bent at the edge of the bed and then raise your arms above your head to get them out of the way."

He hesitated but then inched down, following her directions until his feet touched the floor and his knees were bent over the edge of the bed. Dawn eyed him and then carefully straddled his chest. She looked back over her shoulder, seeing his confused expression until she backed up, her knees ending up next to his chest with her legs spread so her pussy hovered by his chin. His gaze zoned in on her lower half right in front of him.

"Are you getting the picture now?"

He tore his attention from her sex to meet her gaze. She winked and then looked down at his cock. She braced one hand on the bed and gripped him with the other, circling his shaft with her hand. She licked at the head of his cock as if he were ice cream, letting the tip of her tongue trace the ridge of the crown.

His arms moved, pressing against the back of her thighs and then his fingers were spreading her pussy lips open to expose all of her to him. His tongue was hot as it made contact with her sensitive clit. Dawn moaned and spread her thighs more to give him better access.

Iron caught on quickly what the term meant as he closed his lips over her, sucking and licking at the swelling bud. Pleasure seeped through her body slowly, starting at the point of his warm, wonderful mouth and inching upward to her sensitive nipples that brushed against his stomach as she took the entire crown into her mouth, swirling her tongue around it over and over, to tease. She didn't want him going off too fast and leaving her behind since she knew he had been close to release.

Dawn slowly worked him deeper into her mouth but was careful to not suck on him hard or too fast. She moaned around his thick, hard flesh as his teeth scraped across the pearl of her clit that he exposed as he pushed back the hood of it with his tongue. Raw ecstasy tormented her as she started to slowly move her hips against his mouth, needing more, wanting to desperately come. Her vaginal walls tightened and she knew she was close. She sucked on him harder and her lips sealed around him firmly as she moaned louder, realizing he could probably feel the vibrations.

His hands suddenly shifted and he gripped her thighs, lifting her off his body as he struggled to sit up. Confused as he jerked out of her mouth, she turned her head as he put her on the bed next to him. There was no missing the passion in Iron's blue gaze as he sat up on his bent legs. He grabbed her hips and almost growled at her.

"Brace your arms."

She hesitated a second trying to understand what he wanted but then she gripped the mattress, tightening her arms as she locked them straight. A gasp escaped her a second later when his hands gripped her hips, lifting her lower half totally off the bed and then eased her down so her legs were on either side of his bent legs so she sat on him facing away. He shifted his hips, rising. His intent was clear as he nudged her with his cock, it slid in the cream that generously coated her folds from her desire for him. He pushed against her, entering her slowly.

Dawn threw her head back as Iron pushed into her, stretching her and activating nerve endings that were starving for attention. She cried out his name and tried to press back but his strong hands gripped her hips, stopping her from trying to bounce on his cock to get off. She wanted to come desperately.

"You're mine, little red," Iron growled. "And I'm marking you in every way so you know who you belong to."

He started to fuck her hard and fast, his hips become a pumping machine of sure, long strokes as he delved into her deep, nearly totally withdrawing, only to plunge into her again.

"Iron," she chanted his name again and again.

One of his hands slid forward so he could rub her clit with the side of his finger as he continued to hammer her with his thick, iron-hard cock. A scream tore from Dawn's mouth as the climax hit her brutally, ripping through her sharply and made the scream cut off as she lost the ability to breath. Her inner muscles convulsed around his still-driving cock. She started coming so hard she was the one soaking them with her release instead of him.

"Mine!"

Iron shouted that single word as he found his own climax, his body shaking against hers as he pressed his hips tightly against her ass, jerking hard against her as he exploded, jetting out spurt after spurt of cum deep into her welcoming body.

They collapsed together on the bed with Dawn mostly under him but with enough of his upper body shifted to the side of her that she was able to gasp in a lungful of air as she tried to catch her breath. A hand cupped her ass, rubbing her and then firmly gripped her ass cheek.

"That was amazing," Iron said softly.

Dawn smiled against the bedcover. "Little red, huh? I like it."

His hand eased his hold. "I think of you that way sometimes. I let that slip."

She hated to move, so sated in her relaxed state of sexual bliss, but forced herself to turn her head to stare into his face, inches from her own. She winked at him.

"I'm honored that you gave me a nickname."

He laughed suddenly as his eyes sparkled. "It is not as sexual as your 'sexy' reference to me. I thought you would hate it that I think of you as my little red."

"I don't. If I'm little red, then you have to be big red."

The grin widened, creating little lines next to his eyes. "I prefer 'sexy' over that."

She scanned his body. "I do too."

"I like sixty-nine."

"Again, me too. I think any position we try is going to be wonderful but now you know why I was on top."

"I would never force you to take all of me. It would choke you and I'm aware of that."

She believed him as she wiggled around until she faced him. "So do I get to go to work with you again tomorrow?"

"I will if you promise to not attack any more females."

Her happy mood crashed and burned instantly at the reminder of when she'd attacked Fiona. "I can't promise not to if that woman or any other one for that matter tries to molest you. You wouldn't stand there watching a man fondle my muff so don't expect me to stand there watching a woman try to make Mr. Iffy into Mr. Stiffy."

He laughed. "These human sayings are so amusing."

She slowly smiled, acknowledging it was humorous. "Okay, is saying she was trying to put the joy into your man toy better?"

He rumbled as he laughed harder. She loved seeing his expression so open and expressive. He was relaxed and they were both having a great time. His hand rubbed her skin, stroking her lower back.

All teasing left her. "I can't and won't make promises to not hit someone when I know full-well that I will nail anyone who comes after you like that again. If another woman touches you, I'll kick her ass. You can count on that."

Dawn didn't miss the tensing of his body or the way his eyes grew a little cold, his joy fading fast, along with his sense of humor. She'd hit a nerve and there was no hiding it from his drastic shutdown behavior.

"I heard some of what that bitch said to you. What is a breeding pact?" She was curious if he'd shut her out or tell her the truth.

The length of time it took him to answer her stretched into minutes as he looked anywhere but at her. "It just means I've promised to have children."

"So we have to have at least one child?" She was pushing him to tell her all of it, purposely testing him.

"We have to have one child," he said softly.

"So that's it?"

He refused to look at her. "Yes," he lied.

Pain filled her. He wasn't going to tell her about the eleven other men he was in a pact with or what that would mean if one of them couldn't get his wife pregnant. Hot tears burned behind her eyes as she dropped her head, pressing her face against his chest.

"You're the only woman I want in my bed." He pulled her tighter against him. "Always know that, little red," he said softly. "You are the only woman I want to have a child with in the future."

Pulling in a shaky breath and fighting her emotions to not flat out break down and tell him she knew, she swallowed hard. "So you'll never touch another woman?"

His arms tightened to the point that he was almost crushing her against him. "I never want another woman."

He didn't want to touch one but he would, that was what he wasn't saying, but she knew it was the reality of his situation. It would kill her if he ever was ordered to fuck someone else, get them pregnant, and the idea of another woman carrying his baby about tore her up. She wondered how many times he'd already had to do that, how many little parts of the man she loved were out there as breathing proof of what he'd do to ensure that his cyborg people had future generations.

If they returned to his home world, then that's the kind of future she faced. She could run away from him, escape if the opportunity presented itself but the thought of not having Iron in her life tore her up just as bad as the reality that he'd cheat on her one day. She knew he would since Fiona had a hard-on for him. How many other cyborg women wanted to have little redheaded babies? Iron was prized for his coloring. Special. Different. He was a much-wanted commodity.

Iron nuzzled her neck. "We haven't eaten. I'll order us food to be delivered."

She nodded against his chest. "I'm starving," she lied. Her appetite was gone.

Somehow she needed to keep Iron but at the same time protect their relationship by not allowing his people and their fucked-up ways to tear them apart. She wished she could take him back to Earth but they'd kill him there. Neither of their worlds were an option.

Dawn suddenly had a crazy idea but as she thought about it, a plan started to form. She bit her lip, hope and excitement slowly building. It could work. It wasn't as if she had a lot of options.

Iron eased his hold on her. "Let's take a cleansing together. I just linked with the computer and put in a request. Our food will arrive in approximately twenty-three minutes. You may go with me tomorrow but I won't let you out of my sight this time."

"Thank you."

Shit, Dawn thought. He could link with the computer without getting near a terminal. She'd have to think of a way to make it impossible for him to do that. They got out of bed and walked to the cleansing unit together. He was silent, obviously lost in thought and Dawn was grateful. She had a lot of planning and plotting to do but not a lot of time to do it.

Chapter Thirteen

"I had an idea in the middle of the night," Dawn told Iron as they dressed the next morning to leave for the surface of the planet to finish the last repairs on the *Yas* shuttle.

Iron met her eyes with curiosity. "What idea is that?"

"The shuttle is old and a lot of things can go wrong on it. The fact that you have to control so much with your implanted connections bothers me. I know how to find some workable relays for the gravity stabilizer so you don't have to monitor and control them on top of everything else."

Interest sparked in his beautiful gaze. "How?"

"You have emergency pods, correct? Some of them are outfitted with older parts on the nonessential equipment. If you take me and a repair kit to one of them I can open up some panels and try to find some of them."

He hesitated and then glanced at the clock. She knew he was probably calculating how much time that would take. She spoke before he could veto her suggestion.

"I know your shift starts soon but it wouldn't take me long at all. Worst case scenario, the *Rally* has to swing back and get us after they drop off your guys first but it would help ensure your mission of getting that old hunk of junk off the surface to dock it with the *Moonslip*. I think that's worth half an hour of time, don't you? It's only logical to want to do everything possible to make sure something doesn't go wrong. The more systems we have online and functioning on the shuttle, the better chance it has of reaching orbit without a problem."

He nodded and Dawn wanted to jump up and down with joy but she managed to hide it as she ducked her head. "Great."

Fear and nervousness fought within Dawn as they left their quarters. Iron led her to a lift and they went down three floors before it stopped. He walked her into more crew quarters, it being obvious what it was by the lines of doors on each side and their spacing. She saw the emergency signs posted giving arrow instructions on where the life pods were.

A hundred things could go wrong with her plan. She was thinking of every single possibility as Iron stopped next to a pod door and opened up a panel on the wall, lifting out a repair bag. He pressed his hand to the scanner that controlled the lock and the ship doors opened to allow Dawn see a short docking sleeve to the pod. As they stepped into the short hallway the pod doors slid open to reveal a decent-sized, twenty-five person life pod.

Thank goodness for class-A starships and their comfortable emergency pods, Dawn thought, grateful that the ship was large enough to fit her needs. Her gaze darted around the room, taking in every detail and making mental notes of what she could use to help with her plan.

"Where do you want to start?"

"The panels under the pilot console," she said.

Iron carried the heavy bag and placed it on one of the two pilot seats. Dawn opened the bag to remove the tools and light she would need. She forced a smile, hoping he couldn't read that she was up to something when he glanced at her.

"Why don't you go down under the dash to look for older styled relays while I take off the top deck of the console? The wiring is packed pretty tight in there." She lifted her hands. "And I've got the hands for it."

Iron picked up a light source and an all-purpose tool. In less than a minute he was flat on his back on the floor, half his body under the console. She quickly flipped open the top panel. She worked fast, cutting through the computer's connections to the piloting systems. She left it open and grabbed the cutting tool, waiting.

"Can you turn on the power to the controls?"

"Why?" His voice sounded a little suspicious.

"I think I found two relays and I want to make sure they work before I pull them. It's just the screen scanner lights but I need juice to do it," she lied.

The silence was eerie as she waited for him to speak. When the monitors and systems on the console suddenly came on she jumped a little, startled. "Thanks."

Dawn worked fast, slicing through the autopilot that allowed Iron to control the system. Now he would be unable to shut it off with a mere thought via his uplink. She said a quick prayer as she leaned over to grab the emergency med kit next to the pilot's seat.

"Will they work?"

"Yeah, sexy. This is going to work. It has to," she said honestly as she tore open the lid, scanning the contents.

Relief flooded her as she grabbed one of the med injectors all pods carried in case an unruly passenger got space sickness. She tore away the protective covering and uncapped it, glancing down at Iron's legs as regret swamped her. *I don't have a choice*, she thought. She bent and jabbed the air needle med injector into his lower thigh and depressed the release valve.

Iron jerked and his body stiffened as his hips rose until his chest held him down where the console pinned him. Tears filled Dawn's eyes, hating what she was doing. She knew the drug would hit his system fast, because when she was a newbie, she'd suffered a panic attack and her supervisor had jabbed her with a knockout shot. She counted to nine and then yanked the med injector away. Iron's body went totally limp, collapsing on the floor.

Dawn threw away the med injector and grabbed his legs to drag him out. He was heavy and it wasn't easy but she had desperation on her side. She got him clear of the console and straddled him to check for a pulse. Relief hit her when she found it, knowing he wasn't having an adverse reaction.

She straightened, stepped over him, and went to work. She finished cutting all the computer controls first, preventing access to the piloting functions by the onboard computer. She rewired the engine controls directly from the computer into to the console. It took several minutes and she kept watching for any sign that Iron was coming around as she worked. She dropped into the seat, slammed the cover down on the panel and reached for the pilot controls. The engine roared to life as she switched them on.

"Malfunction," an electronic male voice stated as the onboard computer booted up. "Engine misfire. Attempting to shut down."

"You can try," Dawn told it, knowing damn well it wouldn't be able to now that she'd cut the auto pilot connection. She licked her lips as she pushed the release button for the docking clamps.

"Warning," the computer announced. "Docking clamps disengaged."

"Thanks for letting me know." Dawn took a deep breath as she grabbed the thruster control, flipping the switches to turn them on. "Go silent now."

"You do not have access to issue orders," the computer stated. "Warning. Thrusters preparing to fire."

"That's the plan," she stated while she grabbed the twin thruster controls firmly in each hand, knowing it depended on equal balance as she pushed them forward.

The pod shot forward, nearly tossing Dawn back in the chair but she had braced her knees on the edge of the seat, prepared for the jerky launch. She knew that, right now, alarms in the *Star* had to be stating that a pod had just jettisoned away but she didn't want to worry about that.

"Pod 5 is clear of the *Star*," the computer announced. "This is an unauthorized function. Trying to link control access."

"Good luck with that."

She released the thrusters and reached up to open the shielded window so she could see where she was going. Driving a pod half blind and without a computer was tricky but they were in deep space. She'd never be able to pull this off if other ships were around where heavy space traffic existed. It would be too difficult to navigate tightly without the fast calculations and adjustments the computer could automatically make.

"Sending emergency signal," the pod announced. "This is an unauthorized flight."

"They are already aware, I'm sure." She saw wide-open space clear of anything in her path and reached for the thrusters, opening them up, and felt the entire pod vibrate from the full burn she was initiating. The pod launched forward at an alarming speed, her back slamming into the chair. Out of the corner of her eye she saw Iron's body roll a few times but he didn't slam into anything.

"Computer, are the collision senses still activated?" She hoped it would answer since it would be a non-security-related question, one the computer shouldn't be programmed to ignore.

"Affirmative."

"Awesome." If something came into their path the computer would warn her so she was free to move away from the controls now.

Dawn got out of her seat and moved quickly to the repair kit in the other pilot seat. She dug inside and found a cutting tool. She glanced at Iron then nearly ran to one of the passenger seats. He was going to wake up soon and she needed to secure him before he fully roused. She gripped the belts and sliced through them. She moved to the next seat and then the next. In less than a minute she had four lengths of thick belt. She turned back to Iron and went to work.

She secured his hands together over his head around one of the seat legs that was bolted to the floor. The belts were thick and sturdy. She was pretty sure he wouldn't be able to break them. She stood and went to the repair bag and grabbed out a clamper-attachment tool. She crouched and stapled the belt ends together. The clamps were heavy-duty, designed to hold sheets of metal together. She tied his ankles together next, clamping the belt ends to secure it. When she was done she repeated the process, double securing his wrists and ankles. It was better to be safe than sorry.

"Are we being pursued, computer?"

"You are not authorized access."

She hesitated. "What ships are in range? Let's try that one to get around your stupid-ass security measures."

"The *Star* is in range and the *Vontage*, both designated Earth—"

"Stop. I don't want their birth certificates. Just give me distance."

It told her. She nodded and then asked again a minute later. Relief swept through her as the computer told her a greater number. If the ships were pursing they would be closing the distance instead of increasing it.

She pulled up the star charts, surprised that she wasn't as far off one of the main travel zones as she feared. She calculated time and factored in the use of fuel. It would take five days to reach her destination. She adjusted course, deciding manual piloting was harder on long-term flights than just traveling from planet surface to a space station. She turned and gazed lovingly at the big male tied up on the floor. He was worth it.

Dawn removed her boots to get comfortable. She knelt to check Iron again. His pulse was strong. She brushed his hair back and leaned over him to place a kiss on his forehead.

"I'm so sorry I had to knock you out like that, sexy."

214

He didn't answer. Dawn got to her feet to double-check that the pod was fully stocked as they were required to be on all ships. She was happy five minutes later when she walked back to Iron and sat down next to his chest. They had plenty of food and water to last them the five-day trip. She'd barely settled on her butt when Iron jerked awake suddenly.

His entire body went stiff and then he struggled as his gaze darted around the pod, a confused look on his face until he saw Dawn. His struggles ceased and then anger tightened and flushed his features.

"I'm sorry," she said softly. "I hated to knock you out but I had no other choice."

"You deceived me." His voice was ice cold and his beautiful eyes glittered with pure rage. "Have you taken me hostage to make sure my people do not attack the pod?"

"No. God, you are paranoid. Do you always jump to the worst conclusions?"

He struggled against the belts but to her relief they held, keeping him restrained and his arms trapped above his head. His fighting ceased and he closed his eyes.

"Unable to comply," the computer suddenly stated. "Access to piloting controls has been severed. The pod has been stolen by a pirate."

Dawn smiled sadly, knowing Iron had just tried to take control of the pod. She responded to the computer. "I'm not a pirate. I'm a mechanic."

She waited for Iron's eyes to snap open, which they did. "I disabled the computer from all piloting functions. I can hotwire anything with an engine and I can tear out computer controls because I fix enough of the damn things to know how to screw one up if need be."

"Release me and I promise I won't harm you, Dawn."

She stared into his furious gaze. "I can't."

"You are returning me to Earth for death?"

Her mouth dropped open in shock. "Why do you do that, always look for the worse scenario possible? God. Do you know me at all?"

"The female I believed I had correctly assessed would not have attacked me and stolen a life pod."

She moved to her knees and then threw her leg over the stunned cyborg as she straddled his hips and leaned forward to press her hands on his chest.

"I didn't do this to hurt you in any way. It sure as hell wasn't to use you in any way. Whatever you have going on in that brain of yours right now, forget it." She took a slow, deep breath, and let it out. "I know what a breeding pact is and exactly what that means."

He said nothing as they stared at each other but he had gone a little pale. She nodded as she lifted a hand to cup his face, her thumb tracing his jawline. She stared deeply into his eyes.

"I'm just going to be totally honest with you since I stole an escape pod, kidnapped you, and had to knock you out to make sure you didn't turn the ship on me while I tried to steal both of you." She hesitated. "I love you, Iron. I fell for you hard and fast. The idea of you having to touch other women kills me. It will destroy me the first time you leave to go climb into bed with someone else. If we go to Garden, your people can make you

216

follow those stupid laws, force you to have kids with other women. If we go to Earth my people will kill you."

"So your plan was to steal a life pod?" He frowned but something in his eyes softened and the angry tone was gone from his voice. "We can't travel extensively in one of these. We're defenseless, Dawn. We're a target for pirates. This wasn't a good plan to avoid my breeding pact."

"I know it's not perfect," she admitted softly. "But what choice did I have? We can't live on your world or mine but I do know a place we can go."

"Are you thinking of taking me to your space station full of humans? They will see me and instantly alert someone to my presence, Dawn."

"No, not the station. I can't let anyone see you or they will contact Earth Government. I'm not that naïve. The thing is, Arian Nine is perfect."

He frowned. "The planet you are converting for colonization?"

"There's an underground station that isn't in use. When we first set up the scientists miscalculated the changes that would take place on the surface. They placed the Vonder emergency underground station on the far northern region, making it unlivable for nine months of the year. It's an icy area where life would be too harsh. They had me close the station down three years ago but it's totally self-contained and was stocked to sustain life for everyone on Vonder Station to hole up in case we had to abandon it. There's enough food supplies in it to last us five or six years. I'm a mechanic so I can keep it going if something breaks down. By the time we need to re-supply they'll have cities built. I can easily slip into one of them to buy us more supplies without being caught if anyone is even looking for me by that time. There is a three-month window where it's actually pleasant and sunny so we'll have those months to live on the surface to get fresh air and sunshine."

"What about money or do you plan on stealing when our supplies run out?"

"I have been saving all my salary for retirement. I have enough to last us a long time, Iron." She bit her lip. "We can be together, just you and me. I know it won't be easy sometimes but no one can force us apart or control us. You won't have to sleep with other women. You'll be safe from detection right under their damn noses, literally. If you think about it, it's a solid plan."

The tense lines in his features softened. "You would live underground nine months a year to be with me?"

"In a heartbeat."

"Release me, little red."

She wanted to. "I can't."

"Do you think I will hurt you?" He stared at her with a returning frown. "I won't."

"You told me once that you'd lure your captor into believing you were docile and then escape the first opportunity you had. I can't risk that because I'd lose you." She hesitated. "Unless you don't want to be with me. Is that it? Do you feel anything for me?"

Pain gripped her as he silently watched her without saying a word. The thought of Iron refusing to go to Arian Nine with her because he no longer wanted her almost broke her heart. She licked her lips and reached for the tool kit. Iron remained quiet as she opened it to remove pliers. She met his gorgeous eyes.

"I won't force you to be with me, Iron. I love you too much so if you want to be free, I won't keep you against your will." She tore her gaze from his, working to free the stapled belts.

She half expected him to grab her when she freed his wrists but he didn't. He rubbed them instead, still staring at her without uttering a word. She had to climb off his lap to reach the belts securing his legs. She set the tool down when she was done, turning on her knees to meet his intense gaze.

"I guess I should fix the controls now so the computer can take us back."

Iron moved quickly, his hands going to her waist, wrapping around it. He lifted her easily, showing her once again his impressive strength as he set her back on his legs so she straddled him. She was surprised but as she gazed into his eyes she saw no anger there.

"I want you to remain mine, Dawn. You should know that by now. I just don't believe this is the answer."

"What other options do we have? I've been all over this situation in my head. You have a damn breeding pact in your world and in mine you're public enemy number one."

"I was working on finding a solution and have been in contact with two sympathetic members of the cyborg council to ask for their help. Before you took me."

That surprised her. "You were?"

He nodded. "I don't want to be in a breeding pact anymore, Dawn. I don't want another female and I knew, after you attacked Fiona, that you would attack any female who was physical with me. If a human harmed or killed a cyborg, they'd be put to death. I am not willing to risk you that way."

"Why didn't you tell me?"

"I didn't want you to worry."

"Well, it's done and we're free of your people so we might as well give this a shot. We can have a good life on Arian Nine."

"We have to go back, Dawn. We'll return together and I won't allow anyone to harm you or punish you for stealing me and the pod."

"You're putting faith in your council to find a solution for you but look what they did to Coal. Those women turned him into a slave and they aren't going to punish them over it, are they? I refuse to put our future in their hands."

Anger darkened his features. "You do have an obsession with that male."

"I do not." She shook her head. "You're the only man I want."

His eyes narrowed. "Prove it."

"You want me to prove you're the only one I want?"

"Yes."

She grinned as she reached for the front of his pants, unfastening his belt and slowly jerking it free of the loops. "I can totally show you how much I want you."

Iron's eyebrows rose as he stared at her. Amusement spread through Dawn as she wiggled until he released her hips so she could stand and shed her pants. She reached for the shirt but Iron stopped her.

"Keep it on. It is chilly in the room."

Dawn straddled his lower thighs, the material of his work uniform a little rough against her skin, creating an erotic sensation. Her fingers quickly worked the front of his pants, opening them up and then making him lift up enough so she could jerk down both pants and briefs so he was naked from mid thigh to his lower stomach where she pushed up his shirt to just under his bellybutton.

"Look at you," she breathed, her gaze lowering to his erect cock, protruding upward. "I was afraid of this part of you at first." She glanced at his face, grinned. "I never thought I'd have to tell a man he was too big."

"I want you, little red."

He wasn't playing fair with his low, husky tone that turned her on. And he was using his special name for her. She leaned forward as she scooted down his legs, one of her hands sliding up his hip to grip his shirt, which she shoved higher on his stomach. Her palm ran across firm muscles that tensed as her other hand wrapped around his cock. She saw him bite his lower lip as she licked her lips, making a show of it and lowered her face close to his cock until she knew he had to feel her warm breath fanning him.

"You're the only man I want, sexy. I'm yours but you're mine too."

Iron's intense focus shifted from her lips to her eyes, their gazes connecting and holding. "We belong to each other," he said softly. "I can live with that."

She ran her tongue over his cock head, teasing the slit. She shook her head. "I loved it when I was tied down and you could do anything to me. I wish you were still secure so you could know what it's like. Don't touch me and just enjoy this, Iron."

She took him into her warm, wet mouth, hungry for his sweet taste as she started to inch him deeper in. Iron's legs tensed under her ass and he arched his hips a little, feeding her more of his cock as he lay all the way back so he was flat on the floor. She took him as deep as she could and then eased off, using the flat of her tongue and wrapping her lips tightly around his shaft as she pumped him slowly with her mouth. He was so unbelievably hard that she knew he was enjoying what she was doing to him as much as she was.

Her hand on his stomach inched under his shirt, gliding up his rib cage to find a beaded nipple. Her fingernails raked the hardened tip of it, coaxing another groan from her man. She loved that she could do this to him to show him how she worshiped his sexy body. She did.

Her clit throbbed and moisture was pooled between her thighs with each soft gasp and moan Iron made. His flavor teased her tongue with every pass over the tip of his cock as pre-cum eased from the slit. She loved how sweet he was, how good he tasted. She stopped playing with his chest to ease that hand down between their bodies to rub a finger over her aching clit, searching for relief. Pleasure spread through her until it made thinking impossible.

She knew both of them were ready to come so she slowly released his cock with a soft popping sound, breaking the suction. She removed her hand from between her thighs and then lifted up. Iron opened his eyes, his features flushed with passion as their gazes locked. Dawn moved higher, wrapping her hand around his thick shaft as she leveled her hips over him and adjusted him until the crown of his cock slid through her soaked, creamy slit. She was so wet he slid easily as she rubbed against him, wiggling her hips.

"I love feeling you come deep inside me. You pulse and throb, filling me up, sexy."

"Dawn," he groaned. Her name was almost a pleading sound from his parted lips.

She eased down, moaning loudly as he breached her entrance, stretching her and slowly filling her as she lowered her hips, releasing his cock once he was firmly embedded inside her. She eased the rest of the way down until her ass was on his lap, loving how full she was with him right where he belonged. Her gaze locked with his.

"I love you, Iron. I was always afraid to let someone mean so much to me but I'm more afraid of facing life without you. You're everything to me."

His blue eyes darkened. "I love you too, little red. No one has ever made me feel what you do."

She lifted up, moaning at the sensation of him rubbing against over-sensitized nerves in her turned-on body. Pure lust and need flashed through her as she started to slowly lift up and lower, riding him as her thighs squeezed against his. One of his large hands wrapped around her hip to grip her firmly and urge her to move faster.

"Oh, Iron," she moaned as she leaned back. His knuckles pressed against her swollen bud to rub in tune to the motions of their bodies.

"That's so sexy," Iron growled. He bent his legs to brace his boots on the floor and started to power thrust up into her.

She watched him watching her as her vaginal walls clenched and quivered with her impending climax. As Iron pounded up into her harder and faster, hammering her pussy with his unbelievably hard cock, it broke the last of her control. She threw her head back, crying out his name as pleasure turned into pure ecstasy. She started to come, her pussy spasms sending Iron over the edge with her as he groaned her name, grinding against her, coming hard.

Dawn collapsed on his chest, her hands gripping his thick biceps as she panted, trying to catch her breath. A smile curved her lips and she nuzzled her cheek against his shirt, wishing it was against his skin. Under her, Iron's body relaxed as he came down from his own sex-driven high.

"It's going to work," she promised. "We'll be together and that's all that matters."

Iron took a deep breath. "We will be together and that is all that matters. Remember that, Dawn."

His words sank into her brain, something in them not quite right. She lifted her head to meet his eyes. The look she saw in them made her frown. "What—"

"I'm sorry, little red. Your plan is flawed. I understand why you thought it was necessary to do this but we can't go live on Arian Nine. I've been in contact with the *Rally* and she is docking to us right now. You disabled the computer for autopilot but I disabled it so it wouldn't warn you when they locked onto us."

"That's impossible. The computer didn't tell me it was in range so it wasn't following us. There's no way it caught us this fast."

"All the ships are programmed to be blind to the *Rally* in case of something like this. The moment you fled with me and the pod, they were following us."

The door to the hatch was suddenly forced open and four cyborg males rushed inside. Shock held Dawn frozen where she was, straddling Iron. The male closest to her raised a weapon. Fear hit her at the same time the dart did.

"No!" Iron yelled.

His order came a second too late. Dawn slumped on him as blackness rushed at her.

Chapter Fourteen

Bright light irritated her through her closed eyelids and her head hurt for some reason. Her first thought was she'd drunk too much with the women on their weekly poker night. *No,* her mind whispered. She didn't work on the Vonder anymore. She was somewhere else with someone else who wasn't part of her crew. Memory returned with a vengeance as her eyes flew open.

She stared at an unfamiliar ceiling and turned her head, sheer terror filling her instantly. She was in a strange room on a strange bed and as she tried to move, she realized she was securely tied to all four corners, her limbs stretched wide apart. If she didn't think it could get worse, she realized she was wrong as she wiggled to test the restraints holding her. Her naked skin rubbed on the sheet covering her.

No one else was in the room. She lifted her head, taking in the small but nice room. It wasn't a holding cell, she would have expected that but this was definitely a private room and she saw male shirts draped over a chair. Fear seeped through her as she wondered who had her. Where was Iron? Had he given her away to someone? Had someone taken her from him?

She wiggled hard and pulled on the leather restraints. Chains rustled. She couldn't break free.

"Computer?"

It didn't respond. She licked her lips. "Emergency Response." It was the universal code to activate all Earth vessels. She heard a click.

"State emergency," a female auto voice demanded.

"What is the designation of this ship?"

"Unable to respond. Your request for information has been forwarded to the captain."

"Who is the captain?"

"Unable to respond. Your request for information has been forwarded to the captain."

Dawn was frustrated. Who the hell had her? Where was Iron? His cyborg friends had shot her, knocked her out, and it was all a blank after that. He'd tricked her and kept her occupied while the *Rally* had caught up to them to hook them so they could dock with the pod. She blinked back tears. She didn't feel betrayed as much as disappointed. Her plan would have worked and they could have had a happy life on Arian Nine in the underground emergency station. Had he been so furious with what she'd done that he'd made sure they never saw each other again? Her heart squeezed painfully. She loved him.

Minutes later the doors slid open and she stared openmouthed at the big male who walked in. Iron looked grim as the doors closed behind him. He hesitated and then crossed the few feet to the bed, staring down at her.

"How do you feel?"

"Where are we? What is going on?"

He sat down on the edge of the mattress, making the bed dip his way a little. "This is a jumper shuttle we acquired recently from a team of humans who attacked the *Star*. It's designated the *Bridden*. It is state-of-the-art and this is the captain's personal quarters." He turned his head, his gaze flickering around the room before he looked back at her. "They are smaller than the quarters on the *Star* but you should be comfortable here."

Her heart wrenched. "I love you, Iron. I only kidnapped you so we could be together. Please don't give me away to someone else. We're married. All couples have problems but they work them out."

A red eyebrow arched and he reached up, gripping his braid. He slowly started to unravel it. "Is that so? Do you honestly believe I would give you up, little red?"

She stared into his eyes and then saw a spark of amusement there. She bit her lip, trying to make sense of the situation but all she knew for sure was that he was freeing his beautiful long hair. Her attention scanned every inch of it as he released it from the tight twists.

"I made a deal with the cyborg council that I believe you will find more than satisfying."

Her gaze darted to his. "What kind of deal?"

He totally freed his hair, used his fingers to comb it, and then slowly stood. She heard one boot at a time hit the floor as he toed them off. "I'm the new captain of the *Bridden*. We're on our way to Garden where they are going to copy the technology of this ship and then we are going to go on a few spying missions for my people. It will be just you and me, along with a few other males to help run the ship. It will be extremely dangerous but there is special shielding on the exterior of the shuttle that makes us very difficult to pick up on sensors. For leading this mission I was granted a few special considerations."

He opened his shirt, baring his magnificent chest. Dawn swallowed hard, liking what he was saying so far but really loving the way he was stripping. Her heart started to pound and as her body shifted, the restraints pulled on her limbs, making her very aware of her naked circumstances. Her nipples tightened and her pussy warmed with excitement. She was good with math and she was adding up the developments. She was on his bed, tied down naked, and he was stripping. Her tongue darted out to lick her lips.

"I don't mind danger."

He grinned. "I didn't think you would with your history of climbing into oxygen generators and picking fistfights with larger cyborgs."

She wiggled in the restraints. "What kind of special considerations?"

He slid his belt free and dropped it on the floor. "I am exempt from being in a breeding pact, little red. That means no female but you will ever be allowed to use my body as a breeder."

Pure joy slammed through her. "Seriously?"

He smiled. "I have written assurances."

"That's like set in stone, right?"

"Yes." He chuckled. "The only breeding that is going to happen will between you and me."

"Iron," she blinked back tears as she smiled. "That's great."

He nodded. "We're going to be getting closer to Earth than I am comfortable with but this is a good vessel and being together the way we wish to be is worth the danger." He shoved down his pants.

Dawn licked her lips at the sight of a very hard Iron cock. She grinned at the thought, seeing the humor in his name when he was built the way he was. Her gaze lifted. "And what about me kidnapping you and stealing the pod? What did they have to say about that?"

He put his knee on the bed, leaning over her so his long, fiery, beautiful tresses teased her stomach and thigh near him. "You have to be punished for that." His gaze left hers to slowly travel along her body. "They left the severity of the punishment up to my discretion."

Her pussy clenched and her nipples were so hard they nearly hurt. "Really?"

"Yes," Iron's voice dropped to a husky tone. "I believe keeping you tied to my bed for at least a week is a good start to reform you from bad behavior."

"Just being tied down?" She wiggled again, the ache between her thighs turning into something hotter and needier. "I think you should do more than that."

His beautiful blue eyes lifted to hers. "I agree. I think I should fuck you into submission."

"Iron," she breathed his name. "Please? Touch me."

His hand eased between her thighs, which she parted as wide as the restraints would allow. His fingers encountered saturated wetness. His full lips parted and he ran his tongue over them, teasing her with the quick view.

"You need to do what I say and not disobey me, little red."

She rolled her hips, rubbing against his fingers so they pressed her swollen clit. She gasped in a little breath at the wonderful sensation. "Order me to take you then and fuck me. I want you inside me."

A grin spread across his lips. "You are never going to be docile, are you?"

She shook her head. "Nope, but it will be fun to fight with each other sometimes. Tie me down and that's about as obedient as I get though."

A deep chuckle burst from him. "I see I will need to buy more restraints then since we will end up wearing these out soon."

"Buy larger ones that fit you too when you do. We'll take turns on who gets to be in charge."

She saw his cock wave like a sexy flag. He liked that idea or at least his body sure did. Iron moved suddenly, reaching for her ankle. He freed it from the leather cuff and then pushed her thigh up, bending her knee. He moved to lay over her and she hooked her free leg around his hip. Iron pushed into her pussy.

Dawn threw her head back as she moaned loudly at the sudden entry. Iron buried himself in her as deep as he could go and held there until she opened her eyes to lock gazes with him.

"I'll fuck you slow later, but for now, I want you. You make me lose my control."

231

"I love doing that," she confessed. "Take me, Iron. Show me just how much you want me."

"I might not be very gentle." His eyes narrowed and his lips tensed. "I get so excited and you feel so good. I am afraid I'll get too rough and accidentally hurt you. I'd rather hold back than risk that."

"I'm a mechanic," Dawn teased. "I'm tough. I can take you, sexy. I like it a little rough and tough. I especially love everything you do to me."

Iron groaned, lowering his mouth to hers to lick at her lower lip before he took possession of her with a kiss that floored her with how passionate it was as his tongue teased hers. He sucked on her, giving her an image of his mouth doing that to her pussy. She wiggled her hips, moaning into his mouth, wanting him to move and trying to urge him to.

Iron broke the kiss and hovered just over her lips. "You make me so hot, Dawn. You warm me where I was cold once. It's like I'm melting right into you and want to get so damn close that we're one."

"I feel the same way, sexy. I love you." She winked. "Now move, damn it. I'll beg if you want because I hurt for you."

He started to move as their gazes locked together. Dawn's heart swelled with love for the man making love to her. The future with him stretched before her in her mind's eye and joy and pleasure washed through her.

Yeah, I will totally be happy spending the rest of my life melting Iron, she thought.

28010728R00129

Printed in Great Britain
by Amazon